I'll Love You
Till Death

By

She'Marie

Legal Notes

Live

Laugh

and

Love Hard!

SASHA

This man was always freaking late! It was August 8th, and I Sasha Lashey Parham– was being released from a women's state correctional facility; otherwise known as prison! I did a five-year bid for my man, Sean–who still had not shown up, by the way.

You see, Sean was that nigga to see in the ATL, otherwise known as the Dope Man, so I guess you could call me the Dope Man's wife. He was not just a hustler; he was the plug, and the love of my life.

As I stand here and impatiently waited on Sean's always-late ass, I might as well tell you how I got to this point.

To make a long story short, my little brother, Chuck, wanted to get put on. He was only 19, and I didn't think he was ready, but Sean couldn't tell him no. You see, Sean was just sweet like that, and "no" wasn't in his vocabulary when it came to anyone close to him or me. I gave in because Chuck had a baby on the way, so I couldn't tell him no either.

Sean said that this was just going be a test to see if my brother was really ready, so he was only going to start Chuck out with a half a brick and see what he could do with it, and how quick. There was only one problem; Chuck lived in my hometown of Saginaw, Michigan.

Sean had it under control, or so I thought. You see, one of his workers they called Gutta was going to make the run and drop the package off, but he backed out at the last minute. Not wanting to disappoint my little brother, I volunteered to take it, but Sean was not having it. I eventually convinced him that I needed to see my family anyway; plus, I think that really the toe-curling, back-arching, knee-buckling head job I gave him sealed the deal!

I left two days later with my CD case and three four-packs of Red Bull, headed to Michigan. I had this very nervous energy riding me, but instead of taking more caution, I grabbed that half a kilo and stuffed it in my carry-on bag, even though Sean told me to hide it in the secret storage compartment in the trunk.

I woke Sean up, kissed him goodbye, then jumped into my candy apple red 2005 Cadillac Escalade with no makeup, a white jogging suit, some sneakers, and my hair in a ponytail. I popped in my Mary J. *My Life* CD and hit the highway. The ride was actually not that bad. I was making great time, being that I left at 9:00 a.m.; I had only made three stops and it was 7:00 p.m.!

With only three and a half hours to go, I fucking dozed off a little until I caught myself and straightened up, but it was too late. Next thing I heard was "woop, woop!" Damn, it was the police flying right up on my bumper. I was calm, though.

I mean really, I had only been living with a drug kingpin for the last three and a half years, so I was not new to the game, I was true to the game. What I did not expect was for the officer to see my personal stash of cocaine. I was just getting ready to take a couple of hits to help me stay alert right before I dozed off.

Yes, I sniffed a little coke from time to time—unbeknownst to Sean, who would kill me if he found out, but hey, life was a little

8

stressful for me. You try being the girlfriend of a drug lord and not knowing if and when the Feds are going to kick down your door, when you are going get that call saying your man just got locked up, or that he just got killed by the next nigga on a come up.

I slipped up and left the shit on the seat in perfect view. That is one thing about fucking with that shit; it throws you off your square. Long story short, they searched my car, found the drugs, and locked me up.

They knew what time it was because they had been watching Sean and his boys for the longest, and my name had been in the transcripts. The cops did not have anything on them, except for the testimony of a runner he used to employ. He was on trial for murder and trying to get his sentence reduced.

Sean had instilled in me from day one that if you did the crime, you did the time—no snitching. I knew what time it was. I committed the crime of loving a nigga endlessly that I would die, let alone do time for.

I did get one phone call, you know. I used it to call him and shockingly, he told me to tell them that it was his, so I agreed. However, you know I couldn't do that, so I took a plea and got seven to ten, being that this was my first offense with no priors. I ended up getting out early, only doing five years for good behavior.

At first, Sean was mad at me and refused to visit, but kept my commissary full. He even kept the accounts straight for a couple of my new home girls that I'd met; their boyfriends and baby daddies had left them for dead after they caught cases.

HOME SWEET HOME

Here he comes! I am so nervous! Why? I don't know. Maybe because I thought that for some reason, he had left me for dead and moved on by now.

There he was, looking fine as hell in a wet, cherry red, chromed out 2009 Charger with a colorful Swarovski crystal-encrusted license plate in the front that read "Wifey"!

"What the fuck?"

Instantly, I copped an attitude and went off. I could not believe that all of those years, I was foolish enough to fall for the okie doke, thinking that he was mine and mine only. Not only was he late, but he showed up in another bitch's car to pick me up!

Before I knew it, he had scooped me up off of my feet and was hugging and kissing me, telling me how much he missed me. I could not help but to hug him back and tell him the same things. I couldn't believe that after all these years, he still had the same effect on me. He was so handsome at 6'4 with a 230-pound frame, caramel skin and a low cut Caesar with deep waves. All of this fineness and damn, that cologne; I was surprised he still wore Issey Miyake!

Now, back to the matter at hand.

"Sean, whose car is this?" I yelled in anger as I pushed him up off of me.

He chuckled and said, "Baby, this is yours, happy birthday! Now you know I wouldn't let you get out on your birthday without a present!"

Wow, I had almost forgotten that today was my 29th birthday.

"Aw, I'm sorry for flipping out on you. I guess I'm just feeling a little insecure right now."

Sean said, "Insecure for what?"

I said, "Well, damn! It's been five years! You think I don't think you've had another woman by now?"

"Sasha, just get in the car and we'll talk once we get home."

"Alright Sean, but don't try and bullshit me because I will not be left in the dark about your bullshit."

I was sure Sean knew that I had heard about him and other chicks. See, I was cool with that because five years was a long time to go without some pussy. It was all good; as long as they knew that when I got out, they would be cut off!

"Sasha! Hello, Earth to Sasha!"

"What?"

"Was you daydreaming or something?"

"Yeah, something like that."

"You know I love you, right?"

"Yeah Sean, what's wrong? I can hear it in your tone."

"Because I got some heavy shit to tell you that you might not like, but I've got to be straight up with you as always."

I said, "Alright, I hear you."

The ride back to Georgia was long and boring as hell. Sean kept going on and on about this and that, but all I heard was blah blah blah! My imagination was running wild. Could it be he had a bunch of kids, or maybe he was broke, caught a case, or worst-case scenario, he had some type of incurable disease? I didn't know, but whatever it was, I could handle it–I think.

Next thing you know, I was waking up just in time to see the Welcome to Georgia sign.

"The queen has risen," said Sean as I stretched.

"Shut up and get me home! I'm starving!"

"Alright, just sit back and ride, girl! We're almost there."

Thirty minutes later, we pulled up to a two-story brick home in Buckhead, with a garage damn near the same size. To say it was beautiful would be an understatement. It was breathtaking! I got out and followed Sean inside. I was surprised to see that the house was empty.

I turned to Sean and said, "This is nice, but where is the furniture?"

"I haven't bought any. This is our home, and I wanted us to decorate it together. But I did furnish the bedroom for a special occasion," he said, smiling.

"And when will that be?"

"Right now; come on so you can go get in the tub."

When we entered the bedroom, my mouth dropped. There was a California king-sized bed with four posts, a 60-inch plasma TV mounted over the fireplace, and two nightstands on each side of the bed. The room also had a big bay window with a built-in bench, plush white carpet, and red, white, and gold bedding.

The whole room was decorated in red and white with black

bedroom furniture. This shit was hot! I was in heaven, compared to the little ass bunk and tight cell I'd been living in for the last nickel.

I sat down on the edge of the bed, which I had to climb four steps to get on, and waited while he ran me some bath water in the Jacuzzi garden tub.

"Come here, Sasha."

I got up and entered the bathroom, where he had a trail of red rose petals that led to the filled tub.

"Aw Sean, you're so sweet!"

"Yeah, I know! Now get your ass over here and get naked!"

That is the main thing that attracted me to him. He was so damn cocky! I walked over to the tub and slipped my shirt over my head and from there, Sean did the rest. The moment felt so sensual. I damn near had an orgasm, and all he'd done was pull my pants and panties down. Yes, it had been that long. Hell, I had been pleasing myself throughout the years, but nothing compared to the touch and smell of a man!

After he had fully undressed me, I got in the tub and relaxed. About 25 minutes later, I heard Sean saying, "I know you didn't fall asleep in there?"

I laughed out loud. "Yes, I've been dreaming about this moment for a long time!"

"Man, you always got jokes; now get out and come here."

I got out, dried off, and got some booty shorts and a tank top off of the vanity where Sean had left them. After looking through a couple of the drawers and cabinets, I found all sorts of new pajamas and lingerie. I headed into the room and a familiar smell invaded my nostrils. It was Chinese food, my favorite.

"Man, you spoiling the shit out of me; a new car, house, rose petals and Chinatown! Nigga, what you do? Kill my mama or something?"

"Man, shut up and get over here so we can eat!"

I climbed onto the bed, sat Indian style. and started demolishing some chicken lo mein with white egg noodles.

"So, what's up Sean? I can't wait no more," I whined.

"Well for starters, I've been fucking a few different chicks since you've been gone, but nothing serious though; you know that."

"Okay, keep on talking."

"And it's this one broad."

"Hold up, Sean! Don't let me find out you catching feelings for these thirsty ass chicks out here!"

"Hell no, just let me finish. She called me about a month and a half ago and said that she was pregnant!"

I tried calming myself down by saying aloud, "Stay calm! Stay calm! No, fuck this calm shit!"

Before I knew it, I had punched Sean right in his mouth. In return, he grabbed me by my throat and I continued to punch him in his face until he let me go. We both tried the best we could to calm down.

After I was able to get my breathing under control, I sat up and asked him, "Why would you be out here raw dogging bitches in the first place as if you're single? Forget about me and my health, right?"

"Man Sasha, it wasn't even like that, it was an accident."

"So she got an abortion, right?"

"Trust me, that was supposed to be the plan."

"What do you mean *was* the plan? Nigga, you know the code. You mean to tell me that she doesn't know about me?"

"Come on, Sash. Who around here don't know that you're my woman?"

"I can't tell. Yawl apparently trying to keep it."

"Bullshit! I doubt if it's even mine. She claims to be seven months, and I'm pretty sure I haven't fucked her in about nine, so that's why I'm not tripping. I just wanted you to hear it from me and not in the streets, that's all."

"Okay, I hope what you're saying is true because if it isn't, I'm not going to be responsible for my actions, and that's real talk!"

"I feel you, but fuck her and her baby; all this fighting has turned me on. Now, get over here so I can give you a real welcome home."

With that said, he sucked and fucked every inch of my body until every single nerve was ignited. After going at it for about three hours strong and me having multiple soul-stirring orgasms, we climaxed together for the umpteenth time. Once we caught our breath, we cuddled up and drifted off to sleep wrapped in each other's arms.

I woke up to the smell of turkey sausage, eggs, and grits. I jumped out of bed, threw on Sean's robe, and followed the aroma. I felt bad when I entered the kitchen and went to give Sean a kiss and saw his lip. It was swollen with a small split in it.

I started to tell him how sorry I was, but that would have been a lie because I wasn't. That's what he got; he knew that I had a bad temper. It wasn't the first time, and I'm pretty sure that it wouldn't be the last, so I continued on with my greeting and kissed him. I was real extra with it and sucked on his lips to add a little more pain.

"Damn Sasha, that hurt and I know you probably did it on purpose."

I just started laughing, grabbed my plate, and said, "Good," as I left him in the kitchen with his lips throbbing.

Don't get me wrong, I loved me some of him but when it came to being faithful, he wasn't shit!

As Sean entered the bedroom, he said, "So Sasha, what did you have planned for today?"

"Nothing much, just going to see my mama, Ashawni, and a few of my friends. Why, what's up?"

"I got a surprise for you, so get dressed so we can go–" Before he could finish his sentence, I was running my bath water.

"Sean, I almost forgot to ask you, where are all my clothes?"

"They are in your walk-in closet next to your bathroom."

I walked over to the closet and walked in. It was the size of a bedroom and had a built-in shoe rack and wall-to-wall hanging rods. He even had all my clothes hung up and my shoes on the shelves. The only problem was that I had been gone so long that most of my clothes were out of style!

I yelled, "Sean, I can't wear any of this stuff! It's outdated!"

"Stop whining, Sash! I'm going to buy you a whole new wardrobe later on but for now, there are two new fits in there that Shawni bought you."

I started thumbing through the racks and stumbled across some dark wash Rock N Republic jean capris with crystal crowns on the back pockets and a white baby tee with a big crystal crown on the front.

The next one was a light washed jean jumper. They were both very stylish. My sister definitely knew my style. Next, I went over to the shoes and found a pair of light washed jean wedges.

In the midst of searching for something to wear, I had forgotten that I was running bath water! By the time I got to the tub, the water was at the rim. I let some out and got in.

I quickly washed up and got out, then applied some lotion, grabbed a pair of thongs, a bra, and got dressed. I wet my hair and rubbed in some curl soufflé so that it would dry naturally curly, just the way he liked it.

When I stepped out of the bathroom, Sean was like, "Damn baby, you clean up nice!"

I said, "Thanks babe, now what's my surprise!"

He chuckled and said, "Dang girl, you are so impatient; it

wouldn't be a surprise if I tell you, now would it? And we are going to the club tonight, so I'm going to take you to the mall so you can find something sexy to wear."

"What club are we going to?"

"We're going to this new club called Ice, with Shawni and Todd."

I said, "Oh, hell yeah! I can't wait to go out and shake what my mama gave me on the dance floor!"

"I bet you can't," he said sarcastically. "But I'm not even going to trip tonight because I'm just so happy to have you back home."

I said, "And I truly appreciate you not tripping because I just want to have a good time tonight."

He said, "Baby, tonight it's going down. You and the girls can pop bottles, blow trees, and party all night–just like you used to before you left. I know you been on lock with lights out at nine, so if you can't hang then just let a nigga know."

"Boy, shut up; nothing has changed. Just because they turned the lights off don't mean I went to sleep. You know I'm rebellious as hell! I would sit up in the dark half of the night just to prove a point. Everybody thought I was crazy, but I was just sitting up fantasizing about what I was gon' eat when I got out!"

"Man, you are legitimately crazy, Sasha!"

"I know, right! I could never be broken. Be it five or 25 years they threw at me, I wouldn't break!"

"Yeah, that's what your little gangster ass is hollering now, but I bet if a couple of them dykes would've run a train on you, you would be singing a different tune right now."

"Boy, please! I've been there and done that!"

"What?" Sean said as he stopped getting dressed and gave me the side eye.

The look on his face was priceless! His mouth was open so wide that I swore I could see his heart jumping out of his chest.

"Boy, I am just playing with you; you know that I love the D too much for that!"

"Ha-ha! Yeah, you better be because unless I can join, it's not happening!"

"Sorry buddy, but that's never going to happen!"

BACK DOWN MEMORY LANE

When we pulled up to some condos, I asked Sean, "Who lives here?"

"Your mother owns a condo here."

I felt like a kid in a candy store! I jumped out the car before he even put it in park. I hadn't seen her in a little less than five years. She came to see me once when I first got locked up to tell me that I could call her whenever I wanted, and that she would send me weekly letters. She said that she couldn't stand to see me like that and would never come back.

She was disappointed in me. She said that she was also hurt because she thought she'd raised me better than this. I understood, so I didn't pressure her because I knew in my heart, she wasn't built for it and she was right. I was only five after my father died. I was an honor student and always got good grades. I was supposed to be a role model for my little sister Shawni, who was five years younger than I was. I had failed her and my mother.

My mother did not deserve this. She worked very hard at putting herself through school to be a Special Ed teacher from my childhood until now.

Now my daddy, on the other hand, was a straight up gangster! He was tall, dark, muscular, and handsome with shiny coal black hair due to his half-Indian heritage. In the early 80s, he owned an afterhours spot called Club Candy. Candy stood for whatever your flavor of the night was, be it weed, cocaine, heroin, wild women, or liquor–you could get it! You see, when he and my mama met, she was young and naïve. My father was a seasoned veteran, ten years her senior. She went to the club one night with one of her girlfriends, chasing behind some man, and that's when he sweet talked her out of any doubts she had about falling in love with him. She fell head over heels for him very quickly, and then came me; then his wife came, beating on my mother's front door one night at three a.m. looking for her husband! Sad to say, he left with her, but he came over every day to check on us.

Ever since that night, my mama was never the same. Her heart was broken, and my father knew he was to blame for leading her on, but he was a street nigga who couldn't be faithful to save his life, so he showed his love through money and expensive gifts.

I remember one summer morning, my mama got me all dressed up in a purple Sunday dress with some purple patent leather shoes, curled my hair, and put the front in a ponytail with a purple ribbon. She then got dressed in a black dress and some black pumps, pulled her long hair up into a high bun, and we left. When we pulled into a church parking lot in my mama's brand new big body Benz, and all eyes were on us. Me being only five at the time, I didn't understand that Mama was Daddy's mistress and I was his love child, and also his only child.

As she parked, I remembered asking, "Mama, why are we going to church on a Monday?"

"Baby, we aren't going to church; we're going to a funeral," she said flatly.

I said, "Mama, who died?"

"Your daddy, now sit down. You're wrinkling your dress."

I had never been to a funeral or seen a dead person before, so when I saw my daddy in that coffin, I started screaming. I cried off and on for three days straight. I barely ate and didn't sleep without constant nightmares. I didn't even want to go outside and play.

To this day, I still couldn't figure out why my mother told me in the manner that she did, void of emotion—but I would not dare ask because I do not want to stir up any old memories or emotions.

I remember my mom always trying her best to console me. She would always say, *"Sasha, don't cry. Your daddy is with the angels, and he will always watch over you. You'll always be his Sha Sha."* Sha Sha was a nickname my dad gave me when I was born because he just could not grasp the name Sasha.

When I was 15, my mama told me that my father's club had been robbed one night. She told me that he refused to bow down and give up his stash, and went out in a blaze of glory. She said he was always a very stubborn man. Before he died, he shot and killed one man and paralyzed another. I guess that was where I got my gangster persona.

By the time I had reached the door to my mother's condo, she was standing in the doorway screaming, "Sasha, my baby, give me a hug!" She had hardly aged at all.

"Hey Mama, let me close the door! And how did you know I was out here?"

"Sean called me and told me you guys were on the way, so

I've been waiting. When I heard your big mouth screaming at Sean, I knew you were here! Hey Sean, I see my crazy daughter is back to driving you insane, huh?"

Sean said, "Ma, now you know she's never going to change."

Mama said, "I know, but you better stand up to her and quit letting her push you around. I know you love her, but one day you are going to snap and hurt her, and then I'm going to have to hurt you."

I said, "Ma, that's enough, I wasn't screaming at him. I was screaming because I was so happy to be here to see you, so stop hating on me to my man!"

"Girl, who are you for me to be hating on?" she said.

"Anyway, I've missed you so much. How have you been?"

"I've been doing great; the question is how are you doing?"

I said, "Fine, I've just got a lot of catching up to do." All of a sudden, I heard a baby cry.

"Whose baby is that crying?"

Mama said, "That's Chuck's son."

I said, "Chuck? Where is he?"

He yelled, "Right here, punk!" as he walked into the living room.

"Chuck! What's up bro?"

"Nothing, chilling. Sasha, this is my girl Samara. Samara, this is my big sister, Sasha."

Behind him stood a very pretty, petite young woman holding a little boy who looked just like my brother.

I said, "Nice to meet you, Samara," as I gave her a hug.

"Nice to meet you too, and this is your nephew," she said, referring to their baby. "Lil Chuck."

I said, "He's too cute!" as I pinched his chubby little cheeks.

"What's up big sis?" I heard a familiar voice say.

I looked up to see my baby sister sashay into the room.

"Hey, boo, give me a hug!" I screamed. I hugged and kissed her face until she pushed me away.

"Dang Sasha, that's enough!" she said, laughing and wiping her face.

"You know you like it! And thanks for the clothes, I love them."

"Yeah, I started to keep one for myself. But don't thank me, thank Sean. He paid for them."

"Trust me, Shawni, I already did!" I said, smiling hard.

"Ugh, you so nasty!" Shawni, my mother, and Chuck all said in unison.

"Speaking of buying, Sasha and Sean, come on. I'm ready to go shopping. Chuck and Samara, yawl coming?"

Chuck said, "Hell, yeah! You think we came all the way to the ATL not to shop? Mama, will you watch junior for us?"

"Sure, go on ahead and have some fun."

My mom was so cool. She and my sister moved here a couple months before my release for a change of scenery.

Chuck stayed in Saginaw with his baby's mama and baby because he was just starting to make a name for himself in the dope game, thanks to Sean still looking out for him.

Shawni and I both had the same daddy, but she never got a chance to meet him. Our mother found out she was pregnant about a month after the day he died.

My mother started dating another hustler about a year after his death while Shawni was just a baby, then she had gotten pregnant with my brother Charles, Chuck for short. He and Ashawni were stair-steps. His father's name was Charles, and he and my mother married four months later, then they divorced two years after that.

Shawni was my rock, my ride or die. We always had each other's backs, whether right or wrong, good or bad. We were just that tight. Sean knew it too. That was why he kept her close!

MY SISTERS KEEPER

"Man Sasha, did you see the way Chuck's girlfriend was looking at you like you crazy in Saks the whole time that we were shopping?"

"Yeah, that was borderline creepy. What was that about?"

"Girl, when you went in the dressing room, she asked me where you work. I told her naïve ass in your bedroom. You should have seen how big her eyes got," Shawni said, and busted out laughing at her own joke!

"Shawni, you are still a fool! Now you're going to have that girl thinking that Sean is my pimp or something!"

"No chick, you are the pimp. I'm still trying to process how you got Sean to drop the black card. I knew he was getting that throwaway money but damn!"

I said, "Oh, you haven't seen anything yet! I'm about to break this nigga bankroll down so cold, people gon' think he smoking or something!" I joked. "Can you believe he done impregnated some money hungry whore? Shit, we don't even have any kids!"

"Damn Sasha, I'm so sorry I didn't tell you either."

"I know you're not telling me that you knew about it and didn't tell me, Shawni! How much did he pay you?"

"Sasha, it's not even like that! I just found out last month. Sean came over drunk one night tripping, talking about how he had fucked up and some other gibberish I couldn't understand. I threw his ass some covers and told him to sleep it off. The next morning,

I asked him what had happened the previous night and was somebody after him, thinking he done got into some shit. Then he said that he might have gotten some girl pregnant. But on the real, I do think he gave me your condo out of guilt a couple of weeks later," she shrugged.

"No, that wasn't it. I told him that I wanted a house when I got out, and that we would give you the condo after he closed on the house, but you still didn't say why you didn't tell me."

"Because I knew you were getting out in a month and I didn't want you spazzing out and getting in any trouble, delaying the process. That's why! But trust me, later on, I'm going to bring you up to speed, but not now and not here."

"You're lucky I love me some Chinese food or else you would be wearing it!"

"Girl, I wish you would! We will tear this food court the fuck up!"

"Shawni, please. I used to beat that ass growing up, and I still will beat that ass today!"

"Sasha, shut up and let's go find them so we can go."

I said, "Ok, come on; let's go back to the Gucci store real quick so I can buy Samara this hobo bag I seen when we were in there."

"I know I better be getting something too, compliments of Sean's baby mama drama!"

"Sure Shawni, whatever you want!"

Once we got back to the store, I grabbed the bag I saw earlier, and Shawni picked out a tote bag and some shades. The cashier rang up our items.

"Ma'am, your total is $2,146.12. Will that be cash or credit?"

"Credit," I said as I pulled out Sean's card.

Shawni said, "And Sasha, please make sure to tell Sean I said thanks for my limited edition tote and matching shades."

"Girl, forget Sean's whorish ass. He's still on my shit list right now, so leave your money at home anytime you rolling with me this week because he treating!"

Just as I was finishing my sentence, I heard Sean say, "There yawl go. You ready, baby?"

I said, "Yeah. I think I've got enough stuff to last me for a couple of days."

"A couple of days? More like a couple of months, Sis," said Chuck.

"Now Chuck, you know your sister is a diva," said Sean.

I said, "Chuck, you better be quiet because after I teach Samara the game, she's going to be breaking your pockets too."

"Yeah right, she knows better. Sean's the one who I need to teach some thangs."

Shawni says, "Like what, how to be a tight ass?"

Sean spoke up and told Chuck, "Man, as long as your sister keeps giving me what I need, she can continue to buy whatever she likes!"

I said, "That's right, baby! Tell Chuck to quit hating!"

Later on that night...

"Sasha, me and the fellas gon' meet yawl at the club. Shawni knows where it is."

"Alright bae, we will be leaving shortly."

He left, and Shawni and I were sitting on the couch while Samara was in the bathroom when my sister told me some shit that kind of messed my head up.

"Okay sis, back to the talk we had earlier when I said that we would finish later."

"Yeah, so spill it!"

"Okay well, Sean paid me $5,000 to abort the chick's baby that's claiming to be pregnant by him."

I jumped up and started pacing the room. "What the hell, Shawni? I'm fucking him up! How dare he ask you to do some shit like that?"

"Damn Sasha, calm down! She couldn't even see our faces. We wore masks, but Sasha, I thought that I had killed her at one point. I mean, she had bright red blood running down her inner thigh and was unconscious. I slapped her real hard across the face about four times until she came to, and we left! That's why we didn't want to tell you—because I was going to handle the situation."

"So, yawl just left the girl like that?"

"No! I'm not that fucking heartless, dang! We did call an ambulance from a pay phone around the corner from her house."

I said, "Around the corner from her house? Where did this shit take place, Shawni?"

"Now Sasha, you know my style. We pulled a kick door! Sean took me to her apartment in Bankhead, and he kicked the door in. I woke her up with a Jordan to her stomach and continued to stomp her until she stopped moving as Sean stood guard downstairs with twin 357 magnums."

"Shawni, I know that you love me, but you better calm down with that immature high school shit. Karma is real and one day, that could be you. But thank you. Even though I don't feel that it was right, I love you for always having my back."

"I love you too, Sasha, and promise me you will never tell Sean about this conversation. I swore on Daddy's grave that I wouldn't ever tell you."

I yelled, "Girl, how you going to swear on Daddy's grave and tell?"

"Girl, bye. I didn't know his ass no way, so it doesn't count," she said, laughing hysterically.

"So what, he's still our dad, silly!" I said, joining in her laughter as I tickled her.

LOVE, PAIN & FORGIVENESS

About 30 minutes later, we all jumped into the Charger and headed to the club. We were all dressed super fly. Ashawni was rocking a strapless baby blue leather halter dress with some six-inch stilettos, always trying to compensate for her 5'3 frame.

Don't get it twisted—she may be short, but she had a nice round ass, some 36Ds to complement it, a flat stomach, and butterscotch skin. She wore her hair short, dyed honey blonde, and naturally curly. She was the spitting image of my mother.

Now I, on the other hand, was the total opposite. I was 5'7 with skin the color of a strawberry dipped in dark chocolate, with long, silky coal black hair, compliments of my father. I had a plump ass with a nice set of perky 36Cs, and legs for days. I was rocking a one-piece, strapless black leather Chanel short set with matching knee high boots. My hair was hanging with cascading curls and a swoop bang.

Last, but not least, Chuck's girlfriend was half white, real petite, and a true redbone with long auburn hair. She was wearing a pair of red skinny jeans, a gold belt, white halter top, and some gold strappy stilettos. You could try telling us we weren't the shit if you wanted to!

When we got there, it was packed! Ballers, hoodrats, nine to fivers—you name them and they were there. We headed straight to the front of the line after Shawni informed me that Sean owned the club; apparently, this was the surprise he had for me. I had to admit that I was impressed. After we made our way through the entrance, we were greeted and treated like stars due to everybody knowing who Ashawni was.

We made our way upstairs to the VIP section where there was a reserved table waiting for us. You name them— Cristal, Ace of Spades, and Louie V were all being passed around by the dozen. Why wouldn't they, though, with three of the baddest women in the ATL in attendance?

We were drinking, smoking, reminiscing, and having a good time when I saw Sean standing on the wall across the room with some unknown female all up on him. She was whispering something in his ear! I didn't move. I just sat there seeing how far he was going to take it. He was just a giggling, cheesing and shit; then, the chick started discreetly rubbing on his package!

Before I knew it, I jumped up, grabbed a full bottle of Cristal, and headed in their direction. Right before my bottle connected with Sean's head, his brother Todd grabbed my arm in midair and took the bottle from me. He then stepped in front of me, preventing me from getting up on them, so I used my next best weapon—my mouth!

"So, you're just going to be bold enough to disrespect me right in front of my damn face after bringing me here, Sean?"

"Man, Sasha! It is not what you think! You are tripping!"

"No! I'm not tripping, but you will because I got something for your ass! Just wait, you hoe ass nigga," I said as I turned around and began to storm off.

Next thing I know, he grabbed me by the back of my neck and turned me around so that we were face to face and said through gritted teeth, "Sasha, go home. I'll be there shortly."

I came back with, "Nigga, fuck you! I hope that bitch was worth it."

"Man, fuck that broad! I told you it wasn't even like that."

"Yeah Sean, it's like that, and I don't know why you keep checking for these simple-minded groupie chicks. Thinking they got a silver lining in their pussy when you got one laced with platinum right here!"

With that being said, my sister and I exited VIP and the club. By the time we reached the car, the tears that I fought so hard to hold back started to flow like a faucet.

"Man Sasha, you better suck that shit up. You better than that!" yelled Shawni.

"I know, sis. I guess I just hoped he would've changed after all that we've been through these past years, you know?"

"Okay. I feel you. Just because Sean is a man whore does not mean that he doesn't love you, though. He's just got issues and a fucked up way of showing love. It is what it is. Sean's a dog and you're not going to leave him, so stop crying. Pick up your face and let's go back in there and party. Fuck him!"

"Shawni, thanks for making me feel even worse. Yawl can just drop me off and come back."

"Sash, now you know I didn't mean to hurt your feelings. I just can't stand to see you all vulnerable and shit. You just got home. We supposed to be celebrating, not having a *Waiting to Exhale* moment in a nightclub parking lot. Shit! You see where it got Whitney in the movie, don't you? And if you don't remember, I'll tell you, heartbroken and lonely!"

"You are so insensitive at times, Shawni. I'm going home with or without you!"

"Alright Sasha, let's roll because you going to need somebody to keep you from going back to prison tonight."

"You damn straight because this shit is far from over!"

"I got you, Sis. But on the real, just let it go for the night and get some rest so you can get your mind right. And if that means leaving Sean, then do it…I got your back, regardless of the choice you make. And if you decide that you want to kill that motherfucker, I'll help."

"Bet!"

By the time we got to my house, Sean still wasn't home, so I showed Shawni to the red room upstairs and retreated to my own room.

When I got to my room, I pulled out the stash I had Shawni get for me for times like this. I swore to Sean when I was locked up that I wouldn't mess with it when I got out, but I had a feeling I was going to need it; at least for a minute, until I get my mind right and readjusted to the free world again.

I took off my boots and jumper, pulled my hair back into a ponytail, and went into my bathroom to do my thing. I sat at the vanity with nothing on but some white lace boy shorts and a matching bra and poured out that white girl.

I pulled my razor blade and mirror out of the drawer, divided it into three lines, and hit one. The euphoric high that the first hit took me on was unexplainable.

My mind was so far gone that I didn't hear Sean come in and before I could lift my head up from the next line, he had picked me up by the back of my neck and thrown my body into the wall so hard I saw stars. Before I could even regain my composure, he was choking me. It felt like my throat was on fire. I started clawing at his face until he finally released his death grip and dropped me. After hitting the floor, I lay there gasping for air.

Sean picked up my vanity and threw it to the floor, causing my mirror to crash and shatter onto the marble. I looked up, and our eyes met briefly. He looked as if he was possessed or something— like a demon had jumped inside of his body. I didn't know what he saw in mine, but obviously it wasn't fear because he grabbed me violently by my hair and forced my face into the broken glass and cocaine and said, "Bitch, if I ever catch your ass fucking around with this shit again, that'll be your skull!"

He then went into his separate bathroom, took a shower, and went to bed. Twenty minutes later, he was knocked out, and me? Well, I was still lying on the cold marble floor, crying, shaking, and wondering if I could salvage any of the coke!

Once I realized that I couldn't, I slowly got up and painfully walked into the bedroom and got into bed. I curled up into the fetal position and cried myself to sleep.

I woke up around 11 a.m. the next morning to Sean rubbing on my ass. It didn't take a rocket scientist to figure out what he wanted—to have sex, but it wasn't going down! I pushed his hand away and jumped up as fast as my sore body would allow and rushed into my bathroom, slamming and locking the door behind me. I thought to myself, he made that shit up after how he treated me last night. He'd be lucky if he ever got to smell my goodies again, let alone sample them.

I looked in the mirror to survey the damage from last night's festivities. It wasn't too bad, thanks to my dark skin. I only had a couple of small cuts on my chin and a sore neck. I'd survive. I'd had worse over the years…no big deal.

"Sasha, are you coming out soon?"

"Hell no. You should've got some from that whore who was feeling you up last night!"

"Come on, Sasha! It wasn't even like that. That bitch was trying to holler at me and I told her that I had a woman. Then here you come acting crazy!"

"Sean, don't even try to game a gamer. I saw her rubbing all over you and you loved every minute of it, so don't lie because all that's going to do is add fuel to my fire."

"Look Sasha, I'm not going to keep playing these high school games with you. Get your ass out here and talk to me like a grown woman!"

I said, "Kiss my ass and go to hell afterward!"

I turned on my shower CD player and blasted Syleena

Johnson's album *The Flesh* to drown out anything else Sean had to say. I stepped into the shower and let the realism of the song "Another Relationship" make my mind wander even more. If Sean was still ranting and raving, it fell on deaf ears because I was in a zone.

By the time I got out and came into the bedroom, he was gone. The house was so quiet you could hear a pin drop. I grabbed my robe and headed upstairs to see if Shawni was still here. To my surprise, she was up there knocked out with her mouth wide open. I gently closed the door back and tiptoed back down the stairs.

Once I got to my room, I got dressed for the day in some Pink Victoria's Secret sweats, a baby tee, and Air Maxes. I grabbed a set of Sean's LV luggage from his walk-in closet and stuffed it with as many outfits, shoes, underwear, and toiletries as I could. When I was done, I applied my clear MAC lip gloss, then grabbed my black Gucci hobo and car keys and left without any regrets. Sean could go to hell for all I cared! He didn't need me, and I sure as hell didn't need him. He was no longer the man I fell in love with.

I headed to the nearest Hilton, got a penthouse suite, turned off my phone, and went back to sleep. By the time I woke up, it was a quarter after six. I turned my phone on to see that I had ten missed calls and ten voicemails. One was from my mom telling me that she didn't want anything, but to call her back anyway. Two calls were from Shawni, along with a message asking me where the heck I was at. The other eight were from you know who, and if you don't–Sean.

His first message was asking me to call him back. The second was him telling me he was sorry, and to come back home. By the time I got to the last one, I was in tears laughing because all you could hear was Tank singing, "Please Don't Go." Man, that was one thing I was going to miss about that no good ass nigga; he could always seem to make me laugh, whether I was happy or sad.

First, I called my mama and kicked it for a few minutes. Secondly, I called Shawni and before I could say anything, she was screaming in my ear.

"Girl, where in the hell are you? What happened last night, and would you please call Sean's crazy ass?"

When she finally let me get a word in, I told her he had come home and caught me doing lines, then beat my ass and how I got up that morning, packed my shit, and left him.

"Well damn, girl! You could've told me what was going on."

"I would've, but you were still asleep when I got up."

"You should've woke me up. Better you than Sean's stupid ass! He came up there yelling in my ear about your whereabouts when all along, I didn't even know you were gone."

"My bad Shawni, you are absolutely right. I just kind of needed some time to myself."

"Whatever, where are you anyway?"

"I'm at the Hilton in one of the penthouses. Come up here."

"How am I going to get there when I didn't drive? Remember?"

"Take the Navigator. The keys are hanging on a plaque next to the fridge."

"Ok. I'm on my way. I'll call you when I get outside."

"Okay, Shawni."

About 15 minutes after I hung up, she was at the front desk calling me. I had them to send her up. As soon as I let her in, the first thing she screamed was, "Damn, look at your neck! Did that come from fighting or fucking? Because I know you like it rough."

"Shut up! It's not funny!"

"You're right. Aw, come here Boo. Give me a hug."

I said, "That's more like it," as we embraced.

I called in some room service and for the next four hours we ate filet mignon, jumbo shrimp scampi, triple-layer chocolate cake, and ice cream.

Shawni filled me on everything and everybody I'd missed. We laughed, cried, and ignored Sean as he simultaneously blew up our cellphones. By eleven thirty that night, we were under the covers in our undies, hugged up like we did as kids; not like lovers, but like two sisters with an unbreakable bond who loved each other like crazy.

TWO CAN PLAY THIS GAME

When I woke up, it was 10:30 a.m. and Shawni's lazy butt was still asleep. I had three missed calls from Sean. This time, he didn't bother to leave a message. He was really starting to wear me down. I threw on my robe and slipped into the bathroom to call him back. He answered on the first ring.

"Where the in the fuck are you Sash?" he said angrily.

"I'm none of your business," I said in a low, but irritated voice, "And if you don't want me to hang up in your face, I advise you to watch how you talk to me."

"I'm sorry, bae. I've just been so worried about you. You not answering your phone or calling me back. That shit got me stressing."

"Well Sean, I needed some time alone to sort some things out."

"What you need to sort out so bad that you couldn't do it at home, Sash? We had a fight, I lost my cool and did some things I regret, and for that I am truly sorry."

"I've been thinking about me, you, and our entire relationship, Sean; everything that I have been through since day one with you."

"See, that's your damn problem, you think too fucking much! We are fine, and you need to stop trying to convince yourself that we are not!"

"See, that's what I mean, Sean; you don't see past what you want to see. And that's exactly why I can't move forward with you, I'm done!"

"Girl, you've lost your damn mind if you think I'm just going to sit back and let you walk away from me! You are mine, forever! So you might as well stop with the bullshit games and bring your spoiled ass home!"

"Nigga please, you don't own me! I'm my own woman, and I play by my own rules, so game over!"

"You're right, babe. I'm just in my feelings. I'm never gon' be that nigga that tries to control his woman. So really, what I'm trying to say is that I already lost you for five years by letting you take a risk that should have been mine. I can't afford to lose you again due to more of my stupidity. I love you and I need you, Sasha. I'm begging you, baby. Please, just come back home and let's work on fixing what is broken."

I was always weak when it came to Sean, especially on the rare occasion that he got sentimental. My heart really didn't want to leave him, but my woman's intuition was telling me to run for the damn hills because he was probably never going to change. Unfortunately for me, I was a sucker for love. After being locked up for so long, I craved it.

"Okay, look. You know I love you too, so I'm willing to try, but I'm not coming home that easy though. I still need some time to make sure that I'm making the best decision."

"So you're just going to continue to trick off my money on some hotel? Because I know nine times out of ten, that's where you're at when you got this big ass empty house over here!"

"Well, like the saying goes, it's not tricking if you got it!"

"Okay Sasha, I'm going to give you your space, but don't make me have to come looking for you!"

"Don't worry, I won't," I said sincerely.

"Oh, and can I make one last request, bae?"

"What else do you want Sean?"

"I would like for you to meet me somewhere. I just need to see your pretty face. I'm over here having withdrawals," he said, chuckling lightly.

"Look Sean, I will meet with you, but I'm not coming home so don't start tripping once I get there."

"Don't worry, boo; I'm cool now. I just need to see you for a minute, nothing more. So where would you like to meet? The ball is in your corner."

"Shawni and I are going out tonight, so meet us at your club around one a.m."

"Alright, be safe and I'll see you later."

"Alright, bye," I said as I hung up.

As soon as I opened the bathroom door and came walking out, Shawni came running in yelling, "It's about damn time! I almost pissed on myself!"

"I was on the phone."

"Yeah, I know. I heard your whole conversation," she said after flushing the toilet and coming out of the bathroom.

"Damn, you are so freaking nosey. But on some real shit, get an outfit out the suitcase and get dressed so we can go to the mall.

And you're going to have to go commando, which shouldn't be a problem since you don't usually wear any panties anyway, with your nasty ass."

"Excuse you, but I do wear underwear! Well, most of the time; where are we going besides the mall today?" she said as she giggled.

"We are going back to Sean's club. You're not a good eavesdropper, are you?"

"I guess not. Why do you want to go back there?"

"I'm meeting Sean there so we can talk."

"Talk, my ass! You are definitely up to something!"

"Don't worry about what I have planned. Just have my back, no matter what goes down."

"I got you, but don't do anything too crazy."

"Don't worry, I will! No, I'm just playing."

Two hours later we, entered the mall. Our first stop was Gucci, which was my second favorite designer next to Chanel. Instantly, I peeped out this bad ass brown and black snakeskin dress. I grabbed my size, went into the dressing room, and tried it on. It fit my curves like a glove. The whole back was out with a chain enclosure around the neck, and it stopped just below my knees. Next, it was on to the shoes. I spotted the sales clerk and asked her if there was a particular pair of shoes that matched the dress. She went straight to a pair of the same color snakeskin gladiators. They were four inches with a strap that snaked all the way up to the calf, with a snake head at the tip made of Swarovski crystals. She said that they had just got in their new shipment, and I was the first customer with it. I told her to get me a size nine and walked over to where Shawni was sitting.

"So, did you find anything you liked?"

"Yes, I found a pair of silver liquid leggings and a black and silver Signature hi-low shirt. Now I'm just waiting for the saleswoman to bring me these six-inch silver stilettos so that I can try them on."

Just as she was finishing her sentence, another sales woman walked up with a box of shoes. Shawni tried them on, told the woman that she'd take them, and we headed to the counter. The saleswoman rang up my items first and gave me the total. I told her to hold up because that wasn't it. I grabbed my sister's things and slid them over to the sales lady.

Shawni said, "You don't have to do that, Sasha."

I said, "I know I don't have to, but Sean does!"

We both busted out laughing as I handed over the black card, which I had deliberately kept. We grabbed our bags and headed for the nail salon. The wait was only 15 minutes and after two silk wraps, pedicures, and eyebrow waxes, we were on our way.

By 4:30, we were at one of the many Oriental owned beauty supply stores in the hood. I needed to get some rollers, a wand, and several other hair products.

As soon as we got into the store and began to turn down the first aisle, I was rudely bumped by this big ass pregnant chick. Before I could turn around and straight check her, Shawni did it for me!

"Thot, you'd better watch where your thirsty ass is walking if you don't want to feel the imprint of my size eight again!"

The chick just smacked her lips, smiled at me, and kept it moving. I grabbed Shawni by her arm and pulled her toward me just as she tried to lunge at her.

"Girl, that shit was not that serious! Plus, that girl is pregnant."

"Oh yes the hell it is!" she said, still heated. "Girl, that's Amaris, your man's soon-to-be baby mama, from the looks!"

I snapped my head around with the quickness to get a good look at her, but she was already gone.

Shawni said, "Yeah, I thought you might have a change of heart once you found out who she was and why she bumped you!"

"You damn right I do. I'm trying to check out the competition!"

"What competition, Sasha? She isn't nothing but a thirsty sack-chasing whore. The only thing she got going for her is her looks."

I quickly spoke up and said, "Wow! That sounds just like me, minus the prison record."

"Girl, stop! You have it all. Money, intellect, style, and a fine ass man that all these chicks lusting after–including her. She's a thot who already has three kids by three different low-level corner boys. Her vagina's got a thousand miles and counting on it."

"Yeah Shawni, I feel you, but there is more to life than being a hustler's wife. That's not an accomplishment! I'm not trying to be like the rest of these basic females around here."

"What more could you want, Sash? You don't have to work for nothing or nobody. You just blew damn near eight grand on two outfits without a second thought. Who in their right mind wouldn't want to be in your shoes!"

"There's a lot more to life than shopping sprees, fine dining, and clubbing, Shawni. I want children, a career, and a man who's faithful to me. I want happiness," I told her sadly.

Shawni replied with, "If that's what you want then make it happen, and stop waiting for Sean to get his shit together. Find you a new man who wants the same things you want. He's out here. Stop talking about it and be about it."

"Yeah, that shit sounds good, but what about the fact that I got a felony now?"

"Oh, I forgot about that part. But remember, what's meant for you will be. You are very smart, Sasha. I'm sure you'll figure out how to obtain those things and more."

"Yeah, I hope so, Sis," I said as we made our way to the register and paid for our things.

As soon as we got back to the hotel, I took a long, hot bubble bath before washing, oiling, blow-drying and flat-ironing my hair bone straight with a part down the middle.

After I was done, Shawni bathed, dressed and spruced up her hair. We then sat at the bar and drank a bottle of Patrón straight, no chaser and talked about the men in our lives.

After I had caught a nice little buzz, I told Shawni it was time to go because we still had to go by our mom's condo and see Chuck and his little family off before they headed back to Saginaw.

We beat our faces and put the finishing touches on our outfits. I grabbed the bag with Samara's purse in it and we were off. I jumped in the driver's seat of the Navigator while Shawni rode shotgun. Once we arrived at my mother's condo, I grabbed the bag out of the trunk and we headed inside. As soon as we reached the door, it swung open and you know who was behind it.

"Hey Mama, what's up," I said.

"Life. That's a banging ass outfit you rocking!"

"Ma, you really need to stop trying to be hood!" Shawni yelled.

"And you really need to quit hating, Ashawni," said Mom.

My mom was super cool and funny. She acted like a cross between Tasha Mack on *The Game* and Jackee' on *227*. She still had an hourglass figure and could easily pass for our older sister. Yes, Mama had it going on!

I walked in and asked, "Where is Chuck?"

She told me that they were in the den packing up their stuff. I walked back there and sat on the burnt orange leather loveseat before I started playing with the baby and talking to Samara. I asked her if she enjoyed herself. She said yes and talked about how much she wished that she could hang with us tonight, but she had to get back to school and work. I asked her what she did, and she told me that she was a dental assistant and taking night classes to become a dental hygienist. I was slightly jealous because even though I had more than she could possibly dream of at my fingertips, she had what I genuinely wanted—a family and a real job, things I could never possibly have. I was finally starting to believe that there was more to life than being beautiful and the girlfriend of a wealthy hustler.

Their baby started to cry and yanked me from wallowing in self-pity. Shawni walked in, telling me it was a quarter to twelve and that we needed to get going.

I got up and gave Chuck and Samara a hug and kissed the baby. I told them how much I was going to miss them, and how glad I was to finally meet Samara in person. On my way out of the room, I realized that I still had the shopping bag in my hand.

"Oh! I almost forgot, Samara. This is for you. Sort of like a welcome to the family kind of thing," I said as I handed her the bag.

She opened it and pulled the purse out. Her eyes then lit up like a kid on Christmas! She hugged me again and said thank you about four more times. I told her that it was my pleasure, and they walked Ashawni and me to the car. We got in, waved goodbye, and headed to the club.

We arrived at Ice right on schedule. By the time we got inside the club and found a seat at the bar, it was 12:45 a.m. I sat there for about 20 minutes looking for my mark. I turned down drink after drink while Shawni was on the other side of me skinning and grinning with some pretty boy Al B. Sure looking guy.

About ten minutes later, this dude named Malik that I dated for about six months one time when I called myself leaving Sean was making his way over to me. I had met him at a college football game. We got real close, but never ended up having sex for the simple fact that I couldn't get over Sean and slept with him from time to time, and a lady never double dipped—well, at least in my book.

Long story short, I got back with Sean and they had this silent beef ever since. He wasn't a thug or drug dealer. He was a college boy in his last year at Georgia Tech, and first round draft pick for the Atlanta Falcons. He was bred from a well-respected family. His father was a heart surgeon and his mom was an RN, so he had a little money.

He was like a chocolate god standing at 6'2 with smooth skin, pearly white teeth, a broad hard body, and enough waves to make you seasick. He approached me, looking good in a crisp black button-down, some Levi's, and some black Timbs. I zoomed in on the ice in his presidential Rolex and the two-carat canary yellow diamonds sparkling in his ears and realized just how much more he had come up. Just as he had got close enough for his cologne to invade my nostrils, I glanced up and saw Sean and his brother, Todd, walking in.

Sean was looking super fine. He was flexing a fitted white V-neck tee, some True Religion jeans, and some wheat Timberlands. He was also sporting his Movado watch and a platinum six-karat cross chain. He was looking so damn good that I almost forgot the plan until I heard Malik's sexy voice.

"What's up, Sasha; you still looking good."

Before I could chicken out, I said, "I'm good. Let's dance!"

Before he could protest, I grabbed his hand and led him to the dance floor. By the time we got on the floor, they were playing Young Steff's "Slow Juke'n." I backed my ass up against him and started rolling my hips and grinding to the beat. I watched as Sean approached the dance floor with pure rage in his eyes. Right before his foot hit that stage, Shawni stepped in his path and started talking to him. I couldn't make out what she was saying to him because her back was to me, but whatever it was, he just smirked and said all right. He didn't budge though, even after Shawni walked off with his brother Todd. He just stood there mean mugging us.

The DJ must have known I was putting on a show because right after that song ended, he started playing one of my favorite songs, "Make Love", by Keri Hilson. I started winding my body down in a snake-like motion while putting my hands behind me and gripping onto Malik's toned, muscular legs as I rode my way back up.

Sean just stood there in a trance, gripping the railing as I seduced both him and Malik at the same time. I thought, *mission accomplished,* while I sang the words right along with Keri.

"Oh, baby, tonight we gone make love," I sang to Sean to let him know that this was nothing more than just a reality check.

As we walked off the dance floor, Sean grabbed me by my arm roughly, pulled me close, and whispered in my ear.

"Checkmate, now get rid of dude."

I told him that I would talk to him later, and walked off to catch up with Malik. By the time we made it back over to the bar, Sean was standing damn near on the back of my heels. I couldn't even turn around to face him; he was so close.

Breathing heavily, he said, "If you and this nigga don't want to die tonight, then I advise you to follow me when I turn around and walk away!"

Before I could say a word, he turned around and walked away and just like the obedient little bitch I'd always been, I was two steps behind him! I heard Malik call my name, but I ignored him. Shit, the game was over and I wasn't willing to let him get hurt over my drama. I knew Sean's ass wasn't playing. I knew how crazy and possessive this man was firsthand. He had murked niggas for less than that. I was like one of his prized possessions, and he had and would kill for me and over me.

Real talk, one time, me and Sean were just kicking it and I told him how one of my mom's old boyfriends had fondled me as a child, and he had a couple of his boys take a trip up to Saginaw, find him, and cut off his hands and record it as his body went into shock. They found his body behind Miles Liquor Store on the eastside. I know he was responsible for it because I was right there when he gave the order. Plus, I followed the Saginaw news afterward to confirm it. The only thing that I didn't know was what they did with his hands because on the news, they said that his hands weren't found.

There was another time Sean and I were out, and this drunken dude kept feeling on my ass. He kept trying to get me to leave with him. Sean saw him, came over, and checked the shit out of him. He apologized and backed off. About an hour later, the dude followed me to the bathroom and waited for me to come out. He pinned me up against the wall, groping me and asking where my punk ass boyfriend was now. I snatched away and quickly ran off to find Sean. I found him in the VIP kicking it with some of his friends, and pulled him to the side and told him what happened. He told me to stay up there with him and just chill for the rest of the night. He made a call to somebody and told them to meet him in the VIP section. Next thing I knew, his boy Killa Kane appeared, and you could tell some shit was about to pop off by his name alone. The dude was found the next morning with a hole in his face in back of the club.

So, as you can see, I knew how far to push him. I couldn't even say he only behaved that way when he was drunk or high because he only did those things on special occasions. He said staying sober was what had kept him in the game for so long. He always said that it was impossible to stay focused if your judgment was clouded.

We exited the club hand in hand and headed home. As soon as we got through the front door, we were undressing each other. By the time we made it to the bedroom, all I had on was my panties and he was butt naked. He picked me up and threw me on the bed, yanked off my Vicki's, and went deep sea diving like my insides were the ocean and he was a professional scuba diver.

My orgasm came in waves and hit his lips like Hurricane Katrina! To top it off, he didn't even want to have sex. He climbed into bed, pulled me close, and whispered, "I love you baby," and we snuggled until we both drifted off to sleep.

BROKENHEARTED

ONE MONTH LATER...

Sean woke me up and said, "Bae, get dressed. I have a surprise for you."

I loved surprises, so he didn't have to tell me twice! He woke me up at 9:00 a.m., and I was washed and ready by 10:00!

First, we went to the garage where he kept his spare cars. He showed me his old school 1965 Chevy that he restored from the engine to the paint job, which was fire engine red with a white top. I had to admit, that shit is nice! Then, he pulled the cover off my old 2005 Cadillac truck. Man, this brought back so many memories. Some were good ones, and some were definitely bad.

"Baby, why do you still have this truck?" I asked.

"Because I knew how much you loved this truck, so I saved it for you. But I also feel like you have outgrown it so with your permission, I feel that we should upgrade it."

"Hell yeah, what do you have in mind?"

"It's up to you; this is your truck."

"I think I want a Benz, or maybe a Lexus!"

Twenty-five minutes later, we were pulling at the dealership. The moment we got out of the truck, we were ambushed by salesmen. I walked right past all of them and up to this young, blonde-haired white woman wearing a taupe-colored two-piece Chanel skirt set who was leaning up against the wall, and asked her if she could help me.

She said, "Yes, with pleasure."

I chose her because she wasn't pressed. That's one thing I couldn't stand was a salesperson that was too eager to take my money, or that followed you around constantly asking you if you needed help. I also couldn't stand the ones who treated you like you were going to steal something. Plus, men were always trying to get over price-wise.

I told her that I was interested in one of their Lexus coupes and she showed us a couple of different cars, but none of them caught my eye. Just as Sean was walking up, a midnight blue Lexus demanded my attention. I grabbed his hand and we made our way over to it. When the saleswoman made her way over to us, I told her that I wanted it.

The bitch had the nerve to say, "Uh, this car is very pricey. Are you sure you don't want to look at something a little more in your price range?"

I was just about to go off when Sean stepped in front of me and said, "Look lady, if my wife wants this car, then she's gonna get it."

I then chimed in and told her bougie ass, "Look! I don't know who you think you are talking to, but I don't recall giving you a price range. Furthermore, I can afford anything on this lot, so if you don't mind, you can find us another salesperson. Thank you and bye!"

After that bitch picked her face up off the ground, she walked off and sent some middle-aged, balding black guy over to help us.

Forty-five minutes later, we were pulling out of the lot in my brand new, midnight blue, fully loaded, big body 2010 Lexus sedan with custom rims and a Bose stereo system. Now, I really thought I was that stuff. Just like Kanye, you couldn't tell me nothing! Sean was driving and we were headed to see my next surprise when we pulled up to a little mini mall on Peachtree, off of Farr Road.

"What are we doing here, Sean?"

"This is one of the properties that I told you I own."

"Oh, okay. Show me around."

The mall held four different storefronts. The first one we entered was a barber shop. As soon as we walked in, some guy yelled, "Damn!"

Sean told him, "You better watch that shit, nigga, because this right here is all me!"

The guy spoke up quickly and apologized, "My bad dog, I ain't know."

"It's cool, man. She always has that effect on men," said Sean.

Sean then introduced me to all six of his barbers, one of them being as his wife. We kicked it a minute and then we went next door to his restaurant called Almost Anything. He named it that because they would prepare almost anything you wanted. I came up with that name when he first purchased the property and we decided that we were going to open a restaurant. It had a very modern décor with dim lighting, big fluffy couches and chairs with colorful throw pillows, long colorful drapes, tempered glass tables with colorful place settings, and huge vases filled with fresh flowers daily to match. I heard it was hot but as I looked on, I was amazed. He even had a full wait staff, including a hostess and one of the best chefs in the south! He introduced me to the staff as his wife and also their other boss. I couldn't help but wonder who he had to design this place, and why he kept introducing me as his wife.

As we said our goodbyes and were walking out, I asked him, "So Sean, what bitch did you have help you decorate?"

"Now, there you go with that drama! Ain't nobody help me because I hired an interior decorator, which I already told you before I even opened it!"

"I know, baby. I guess I'm just a little jealous because you did everything without me."

"Sasha, that's not true. Even though you were locked up, you contributed a lot to our growing empire. And lately, all you've been talking about is going to school and working, so I decided to help you start making that a reality."

"What do you mean by that, Sean?"

"Turn around, Sasha!"

"What?"

"Just lose the attitude girl, and turn around!"

I stopped and turned around to see a vacant space for rent.

"Okay Sean, what are you going to do with this one?"

"No, Sasha. The question is what are you going to do with it?"

I was so blown away I couldn't speak, and that was rare for me!

When I finally found my voice, I said, "Thank you, baby! I'm so happy! I don't know

what to say!"

"Don't say anything. Just go in and check it out."

He handed me the keys and I unlocked the door and walked in. It was very spacious and clean. I said to myself, "*Yeah, I can work with this.*"

"So Sasha, have you decided what you're gonna do with it?"

"Yeah. I think I'm gonna open a beauty shop."

"Okay. I can see that, but you can't do no hair, Boo."

"Ha, ha! Very funny, motherfucker! I ain't talking about me doing hair. I'm going to hire some beauticians, and maybe a nail tech."

"My bad, Boo. I ain't know. You ready to ride?"

"Yeah, boy. Let's go. I'm so hungry my stomach is touching my back!"

"Sash, you want to go next door and get something to eat?"

"Nah. I'd rather go home and cook me some turkey bacon and some veggie and cheese omelets."

"Well, let me hurry up and get you home. Shit, I don't know what I missed most, you or your cooking!"

"It better be me, punk!" I said as I playfully gave him a gut shot.

We spent the rest of the day cooped up in the house after we got home and ate. We shared the day watching movies and eating junk food, and ordering our furniture for the living and dining rooms. We were watching one of my favorite movies, *Sparkle*. It was right at the part when Sister died, singing all drugged out on that stage, and I was crying like I always did when I watched that movie.

Right then, Sean decided to drop another bomb on me. He told me ole girl called him from the hospital and told him that she had gone into labor. She had a premature baby boy and told him that she had named him Sean, Jr. I was so hurt and beyond words that I just tuned whatever else he said out. I couldn't believe what I was hearing. I wished, at that moment, that my sister would have killed that bitch and her baby that night! I'm sorry, but that's just how I felt. Sean was mine, and I was supposed to be his wife and have his first child.

At that moment I couldn't even stand to look at Sean anymore. I heard him calling my name and snapped out of the trance I was in. He was saying how he felt like going up there and killing that ho when she said what she had named that baby. He also said he was so sorry for hurting me by sleeping with her, but that he was 100% positive that bastard wasn't his. He told how he was gonna hunt that bitch down and pay for her to take a paternity test ASAP and squash this shit. I was crying so hard I couldn't see. Sean tried to console me, but I wasn't buying it.

I jumped up and told that nigga, "I want to kill you and that bitch right now!"

He just looked at me as if I had lost my mind, and that just enraged me even more. I grabbed my lamp and tried to take that nigga's head off with it. When he ducked, the marble lamp hit the wall and shattered, then I really lost it! I went into my nightstand drawer and pulled out my pearl-handled chrome .357 and aimed it at that nigga's head, and told him to get the fuck out. He got up and walked toward me.

I cocked it back and said, "You got two seconds to get yo lying, cheating, sorry ass out or I'm gonna pull this trigga!"

He didn't protest anymore. He just got up and threw on a t-shirt, some jeans and sneaks with no socks, grabbed a stack off the dresser, then got his keys and left. Once I heard the door slam, I dropped the gun down to my side and sighed. I then put the gun back in the drawer. I was so tired of living like this. I didn't know what to do. I mean, I loved him, the money, the cars, jewelry, and extravagant trips, but was it worth the bitches, babies, drugs, and abuse? I used to think it was until I went to prison and had nothing but time to think about the lifestyle that I led, and the consequences it brought.

It hadn't always been like this, though. Sean was so attentive and sweet at first. Over the years, he had hardened. I remember when we first met. I was so naïve that I hadn't even lost my virginity yet. I was almost 23 and was in Atlanta partying with a old high school friend name Onna.

We hit club after club until the wee hours of the morning. Afterward, we decided to go to the Waffle House. We ordered our food and found a table. Onna and I were laughing and enjoying each other's company when Sean and his brother Todd walked up to the table. Sean was the first to speak. He asked for my name and number, and I obliged. For the next six months, we spent endless amounts of time on the phone and he flew me back and forth. We made it official on our six-month anniversary and I flew in to meet his parents. His father owned a construction company and his mother was an accountant. They were very nice people, and we hit it off swell.

I later learned that Sean had dropped out of school in the 11th grade and started selling drugs. His only sibling, which was his younger brother Todd, graduated. He followed in his brother's footsteps and started working for him. They were two years apart, grew up in Buckhead, and went to a private school. He has always been a bad boy, and I guess it was finally starting to affect me as well.

Now it was like the more I went through, the more I wanted to change and be a better person. Even though I wanted Sean to leave, a part of me wished he would walk back through that door and hold me while I cried myself to sleep. Maybe it was because I knew he was probably in another bitch's bed by now.

I went over to my TV and put in my Teedra Moses CD so the surround sound could drown out the thoughts in my head. I got under the covers and grabbed one of Sean's pillows so I could at least have his scent along with the sounds of "No More Tears" to put me to sleep.

The next morning, I awoke to an empty bed and Teedra singing about some nigga's backstroke. No matter how bad I wanted to, I refused to call or text Sean. I dragged myself out of bed and went downstairs to our bar/night club, which spanned of our whole basement. That was Sean's personal space that he used for entertaining and business purposes. It had a stage with a pole, a disco ball, a dance floor, a wraparound electric blue leather sofa, a full bar with a couple of silver tables and electric blue leather chairs, mirrored walls from the floor to ceiling, and a DJ booth!

I made my way over to the bar and grabbed a fifth of Patrón and a glass, and headed back up the stairs. When I got upstairs, I dropped in two lemon wedges, then headed back to my room. I walked over to the TV and removed Mrs. Moses and replaced her with Mrs. Blige's *My Life* CD. I pulled the drapes tight, turned off my phone, and got back in the bed. Before I knew it, I had downed half of the bottle and passed out.

When I woke up again, it was 6:00 the next evening. My head was pounding so hard. I got up and found a bottle of Aleve, took two, and laid down and went right back to sleep. I continued this process for three days, replacing the Patrón with weed, and then coke; I replaced out *My Life* with *Share My World,* then *The Breakthrough*, and still no Sean.

By the fourth day, I was so gone and delusional that I didn't know whether I was coming or going. I hadn't bathed or eaten once since the day he left, and it was starting to take its toll on me, so I decided to go in the kitchen and grab a couple of slices of bread and some water to fill me up and then take a shower. As soon as my feet touched the floor, I felt my insides rising up my throat. I raced to the bathroom and plunged my head into the toilet and let it go. I threw up until I was dry heaving and my veins were popping out of my head. My stomach was in excruciating pain, almost unbearable. I felt dizzy and sweaty, and the banging in my head was so loud that I thought it was real. In all actuality, it was real! I realized that when I was crawling back to the bed. I saw Shawni's face standing over me right before I passed out.

I HATE THAT I LOVE YOU

When I came to, I was hooked up to all kinds of tubes, monitors, and an IV. I looked around, and no one was there but me. I didn't remember how I got there until I saw Shawni walking through the door.

Her first words were, "Sha, what the fuck is wrong with you? You could've died or killed my niece or nephew, and over a man, at that! You are a real dummy!"

I wanted to jump out of that bed and put a hurting on her ass, but my body wouldn't allow it. I took a sip of water from the cup sitting on the tray table and told her to get out. She told me she wasn't going anywhere and sat down right next to me. I calmly asked her why she wouldn't leave.

"Sha, I'm not leaving until Mommy gets here. And why you ask? Because I'm your sister, and I love you."

"If you love me so much, then why are you talking to me all greasy like that?"

"Sha Sha, you really scared me. I kept calling your phone and getting no answer. I just figured that ya'll was bae'd up and didn't want to be interrupted. After the third day, I called Sean's phone and he told me what had happened. He said he tried calling but you didn't answer, so he had got himself a room at the Marriott until you'd calmed down. And on the fourth morning, when your phone went to voicemail, I was on my way. I tried ringing the doorbell but your music was so loud that I figured you couldn't hear me anyway, so I used my key and let myself in. When I found you, you were passed out on the floor in front of your bathroom in nothing but your bra and panties! I called an ambulance, and that's why I'm so pissed at you. Sasha, you could have come to me. I'm your sister. We can get through anything together."

I laid back and let the tears that I had bottled up flow. Shawni came over and embraced me, and we held each other and cried until Sean walked in. Shawni reluctantly got up to leave and give us some privacy. She gave Sean the evil eye on her way out. Sean hesitantly came and sat on the bedside. He hugged me and told me how much he loved me, and how sorry he was for all the hurt that he had caused me. He then asked me if I was okay, and why I didn't tell him I was pregnant? My mind went back to what Shawni said about being an aunt.

I said aloud, to no one in particular, "I'm pregnant?"

Sean said, "You mean to tell me you didn't know?"

"No, baby! Honestly, I didn't. But I guess we have been fucking like jack rabbits since I came home." He told me that the doctor said that I was dehydrated and was starving the fetus, and that I was only about four weeks pregnant and how surprised they were that it made it. I spent the next three days in the hospital and was sent home with an appointment with a substance abuse clinic. Sean took me home and waited on me hand and foot for the next week, and on that eighth day, it was back to business for him and me.

My shop was decorated in purples and metallic silver. I hired four beauticians: Chanel, Christian, Kiea, and my cousin Krystal, who had just graduated hair school. I also hired two nail techs, Karla and Tiara, and Sean's little cousin Tyra as the shampoo girl. Shawni was my secretary and bookkeeper. She was smart as hell, but wouldn't apply herself for shit. She would always say that her only job was pimping niggas, and that she had the only degree she would ever need, and it was called pimpinology!

My shop was going to officially be open for business the following week. Sean had taken his DNA test and we were waiting for results. I was shocked that the bitch actually showed up. He paid $450 to an agency called DNA Diagnostics. I was happy to be pregnant, but still a nervous wreck waiting for the results of Sean's paternity test. I so desperately wanted our baby to be his first, and if it wasn't, that bitch and Sean was gonna have hell to pay! I knew that was wrong, but fuck that! After all, I'd gone through fucking around with Sean's no-good ass, I'd be damned if I'd let another bitch come through and steal my shine! Shit, him having another baby would only take money out of my pockets, Gucci off of my feet and shoulders, and steak and lobster out of my mouth. Most importantly, my baby would have to share her daddy with some other little bastard!

A couple of weeks after the shop opened, I was awakened by Sean telling me to get up because we needed to talk. I reluctantly got up and went to the bathroom and peed, washed my face, and brushed my teeth.

When I returned to the room, Sean was sitting on the edge of the bed holding some papers in his hand. I walked over to him, stood in-between his legs, and asked, "What's this?"

"Read it and see," he told me.

I unfolded the papers and read the first one, and out of all the words on that paper, my eyes instantly zeroed in on the words saying that Sean was 99% excluded as the father. I was so happy that the tears immediately began to pour.

Sean said to me, "Baby, why are you crying? You should be happy!"

"I am! It's just that it feels like a huge burden has been lifted off my shoulders!"

Sean picked me up and sat me on his lap and said, "There's something else I need to talk about."

"What is it, baby?"

"Well Sash, lately, I've really been thinking about you and our baby."

"Don't tell me you want me to get rid of it Sean, because you promised me the last time that you would never ask me to do that again. You know how hard that was for me, but I sacrificed my beliefs to show you how far I was willing to ride for you. So please don't put me through this again!" I went to get up and Sean grabbed me and held me down.

"Calm down Ma, and listen. I ain't even on it like that no more. I love you girl, and I

want this baby just as much as you do. I was young and immature back then. I'm on my grown man now! I was gonna ask you, did you try to kill yourself on purpose? And I also wanted to let you know that I would totally support you in whatever decision you made, as long as it didn't involve you hurting yourself again."

"Baby, I was just going through it at the moment, and one thing led to another. But I didn't do that shit on purpose. I was mad at you and missing you at the same time. I just wanted the pain to go away."

"Sasha, you should have called me. I would've come back. I never should have left you in that state of mind in the first place. But I'll always be here for you, whenever you need me. I'm sorry I hurt you. You're my soulmate. My heart won't beat without you, baby."

"Sean, I know it was hard being out here with me being locked up with all this temptation and pussy out here, so I can't blame you too much for fucking those hoes, but getting them pregnant is unacceptable."

"I know, Ma. I fucked up. We dodged that bullet and I swear, this will never happen again! Now, get up. Daddy gotta go make some money!"

"Daddy, nigga please! We ain't had the baby yet!"

"Girl, shut up and find me something to wear while I jump in the shower."

I went to Sean's walk in-closet and flipped the switch on the electronic clothing rack, and stopped it at a pair of freshly dry cleaned Prada dark washed jeans with a crisp red short-sleeved Prada shirt. I walked over to his shoe racks and grabbed his red crocodile leather tennis shoes with the navy soles. I went and made my bed, then grabbed the shit and set it on the bed. I went into my walk-in closet, turned on my rack, and stopped on a short-sleeved, dark purple sequin tunic paired with matching liquid leather leggings.

I turned off the rack, grabbed my outfit, then went over to my built-in shelves. I grabbed my small black leather signature Chanel hobo bag and my new, fresh in the box exclusive dark purple Chanel ankle boots.

By the time I came out, Sean was at the front door yelling, "Sasha, I'm gone!"

I jumped in the shower, washed my body and hair, and got out. I put some Jam on my edges and pulled my hair back into a sleek ponytail and scrunched my ponytail with some Herbal Essence mousse.

I then rubbed some Palmer's Shea Butter lotion all over my body, got dressed, sprayed on some Envy by Gucci, and applied some lip gloss, eye shadow, and mascara. I slipped into my boots, a pair of medium-sized diamond hoops, and went into the kitchen and fixed me a bowl of Golden Grahams.

I stood at the cabinet and ate my cereal. After I was done, I transferred my stuff from one purse to the other. I grabbed my keys, set the alarm, jumped into my car, and headed to the shop.

When I got there, it was business as usual. By the end of the day, I was so mentally and physically tired from helping the girls and getting my money in order that I just wanted to go home and go to bed. It was about 10:00 at night, and me and Shawni were the only two still at the shop and the strip mall period.

"Alright, Sha Sha. I'm finally done. You ready?" asked a sleepy Shawni.

"Yeah. Turn them lights off over there and get our bags while I go close the blinds and set the alarm."

"Okay. I'm right behind you."

Once we got outside, I went to lock the door when three niggas in black ski masks and black jogging suits cornered us. Shawni tried to run when one of the niggas grabbed her by the back of her shirt and pushed her into the shop, where the other two niggas already had me with a .357 to my head making me disarm the alarm. The one nigga threw my sister in a corner and one of the two threw me in one of the salon chairs.

I yelled to him, "Take whatever ya'll want! Here's my purse. There's over $400 and some credit cards in there. Yawl can have it all. Just please let us go!"

"Shut up, bitch! We don't want your money!"

"Well, what you want then?"

"You! Now shut up and turn around!"

"What, nigga? Is you crazy? Do you know who my–"

Before I could finish my sentence, I felt the butt of his gun knock one of my front teeth out. That shit hurt so bad that I couldn't scream, but Shawni sure as hell did before she caught three gut punches from the nigga who was holding her. I told her to just stay calm, and that I was all right. Then, one of the dudes grabbed me while the other one ripped my leggings and lace boy shorts off. He threw me onto the floor, grabbed me by my hair, and rammed his dick in my mouth. He was ramming it in and out so fast that I couldn't even bite it.

The other one lifted me up and held me while he rammed his dick in my ass. I had gotten so numb to the pain that I'd zoned out until I was snapped back into reality by Shawni's screams. As the tears streamed down my face, all I could think of was the terrified look that was plastered across her face when I looked up. Just when I thought I was going to pass out, they pulled out one at a time, and took turns spitting their nut all over my face, hair, and ass.

They were laughing and calling me super head, amongst other degrading names. I thought it was over until the other nigga that was holding Shawni switched places with the one who had violated my ass and shoved his dick in it.

Luckily for me, he was much more excited than the first one, so he came very quick and when he did, he pulled it out, covered in my blood, and forced it into my mouth to relieve his sperm. When he pulled out, I was so disgusted that I started throwing up blood and nut and everything I had eaten that day. When I was able to stop vomiting enough to lift my head, I saw Shawni running over to me as the nigga was leaving out.

The last one stopped at the door and as he walked out said, "Hoe, tell yo man that that was for fucking over my sister!"

Shawni jumped up and ran to lock the door. She then took out her cell phone and called an ambulance, then I heard her frantically yelling to Sean that I had been raped and to come now. He must have been asking her by who because she said that she didn't know, and then repeated what the nigga told me on the way out. She then yelled at him to hurry up and hung up the phone. Shawni grabbed some towels and wiped my face off and covered my bottom with the rest.

"Are you all right, honey?"

"I'm fine, Ashawni. Just sore as fuck. But I feel like I'm going to pass out."

"Just hold on. Sean and the ambulance are on their way."

We both jumped when we heard someone banging on the door.

"Shhhh! Don't say a word," I whispered to Shawni.

The banging was persistent and then I heard Sean yelling, "It's me, baby! Open up!" I tried to stand, but my legs were too weak.

Shawni said, "Sha, don't move. I'll get it."

As soon as she opened the door, Sean ran over to me and picked me up, and sat down on the silver secretary desk; he asked me who had done this to me and I shook my head, saying that I didn't know, but that there were three of them. He kissed me on my forehead and told me that he loved me, and that he was gonna personally body all them muthafuckas!

I heard sirens and a couple of seconds later, the paramedics knocked on the door and Shawni let them in. They asked me if I could walk. I shook my head no, and then Sean said that he would carry me. The female paramedic then left and returned with a blanket and covered me up. Sean walked me to the ambulance and stepped up inside. He placed me on the gurney and let one of the paramedics check me over while the other one was out there checking Shawni over. I saw Sean walking off and I called his name. He walked back over to me.

"Baby, I'm gonna be right behind you. You'll be okay. Shawni's going with you."

"No, Sean! I need you! You promised me you'd always be here when I needed you, and baby, I need you more than anything in the world right now!"

"Sean, it's okay. You go and comfort her. I'll follow yawl."

"Alright Shawni, but are you sure you're okay? You sure you are not too shaken up to drive?"

"Yeah boy, I'm fine. Just go and take care of my big sister."

Sean got in and held my hand the whole way. He didn't speak, but I could see the rage in his eyes. Once we got to the emergency room, I was taken back while Sean and Shawni stayed in the waiting room. After I had been checked over with the rape kit and tested for HIV and any other sexually transmitted disease known to man, I was thoroughly questioned by the police for about 20 minutes. After that, Sean and Shawni were allowed in.

The nurse helped me shower and get into the bed. I was so exhausted that I could barely keep my eyelids open. I heard Sean call his brother Todd and tell him to come and pick Shawni up and stay the night with her, and that he would explain the situation later. Todd was there within 15 minutes and they met him at the door. I don't know what was said, but Shawni kissed me goodbye and left. Sean came back into the room, then climbed in the bed behind me and I flinched.

"Baby, it's okay," he said as he pulled me closer. "I won't hurt you, and I'll make sure no one else will. Just relax and go to sleep. I got you."

I had to stay overnight over night for observation. The next thing I knew, I was waking up to a nurse checking my vitals and giving me some pain medication. I started to panic, asking where Sean was.

When I heard him say, "I'm right here, baby. Calm down," I looked to my left and there he was, sitting in the recliner chair. I took a deep breath, exhaled, and let the nurse do her job. After she was done, I laid back down and drifted back off. I was awakened by Sean's strong hand gently squeezing my shoulder. I opened my eyes and he was standing there with the same doctor that I had seen the night before. I glanced at my Cartier watch to see that it was only 7:00 a.m.

I sat up straight and said to the doctor, "Good news or bad?"

He said, "Ms. Parham, all your tests came back negative with the exception of the HIV test, which we won't have the results to for a couple of weeks. We will contact you when they're in."

"What about the baby?" Sean asked.

"Well, luckily the baby was not harmed, but I'm going to need you to keep her off her feet for about a week. And I'm going to need you to make sure that you keep and attend all of your doctor appointments for further monitoring. Also, as far as the stitches go, they will dissolve. For discomfort, you may use Tucks pads, which you can find at any drugstore. With that said, one of the nurses will be in shortly to unhook the monitors and have you sign your discharge papers. Then, you will be free to go."

"Thank you, Dr. Bush." With that said, he left.

I turned to Sean and said, "Baby, I need something to wear. I can't put those clothes back on!"

"I know, baby. I threw those away. I just didn't want to leave until after the doctor came in."

"I understand."

"Okay. I'm gonna run home and grab you something. What should I get?"

"Look in my bathroom and on those shelves on the wall. I have some sweat suits. And in the drawers below it, there are underwear and ankle socks. And grab me some sneaks out of my closet."

"Anything else, Sash?"

"No. I mean, yeah!"

"What girl?"

"Do not get any thongs either!"

"I won't. Now sit back and chill. I'll be back."

Sean was back in 45 minutes, and by then I had been discharged. He helped me get dressed, and we left and headed for home. I was so glad to see my house. I wanted to jump for joy and

I would have too, if my body wasn't so sore.

Once we got into the house, Sean ran me a bubble bath, helped me get undressed, and picked me up and sat me in the tub. What he did next shocked the shit out of me. He asked me to lay back, and I did. He started with my hair. He already had the Motions shampoo and conditioner, and the Baby Phat Goddess bath and shower gel sitting on the side of the tub.

He washed me from head to toe. He then wrapped my hair up in a towel and helped me stand up, then he dried me off with another towel and wrapped me up in it. He carried me from the bathroom to the bed. He unwrapped me and rubbed my body from the neck down with the matching Baby Phat Goddess lotion. He had one of my t-shirt gowns lying on the bed, which he picked up, then removed the towel from my head and slid the gown on. He got up and went back into the bathroom. Sean had already turned the bed down, so I climbed underneath the covers. He returned with a brush and a ponytail holder. I chuckled and sat up straight, then he chuckled and proceeded to brush my hair into a ponytail. When he was done, he showered and threw on some boxers and climbed into the bed behind me. I lay there, wrapped in his arms, both of us laying there silently and drowning in our thoughts for about an hour, until our minds were so exhausted that we both fell asleep.

HELL AND BACK

The next couple of days were the worst. I slept all day off and on and because of that, I had to sneak and take sleeping pills to sleep at night. I would wake up gagging and sweating, two and three times a night. Sean would wake up and try to console me, but I just couldn't shake the nightmares. It was like every time I closed my eyes, all I could see was big black dicks coming toward my face, and sometimes there would be a whole lot of bright white teeth dancing to the sound of laughter in a pool of blood. Sean was being very attentive and patient with me, but I knew he was getting tired of my bullshit.

I barely ate anything and when I did, I'd throw it up because for some reason, everything reminded me of or tasted like cum to me. Sean would try his best to convince me that it was all in my head, but to me it, felt real, no matter what he said. Once he saw that his convincing wouldn't work, he got fed up and started threatening to leave me if I didn't at least eat three meals a day. I tried forcing the food down and sneaking to throw it up, and it seemed to be working because Sean was the happiest that I had seen him over the last week, but eventually, that all had come to an end.

One night, I was in such a hurry that I forgot to lock my bathroom door. I must have been in there a little too long because Sean came and knocked on the door to ask if I was all right; when I didn't answer, he barged in and caught me leaning over the toilet with a bath towel clenched to my mouth. I had been throwing up in the towel to muffle the sound so Sean wouldn't hear it and would think I was just using the bathroom or whatever. He started yelling out shit like he couldn't deal with this shit no more, and how I had to pull it together on my own because he was done with me.

I started screaming back, "Well leave then, motherfucker! I don't need you! Better yet, we don't need you!"

"We, we Sasha? You've got a lot of nerve saying that shit. You don't give a fuck about that baby because if you did, you wouldn't be doing this shit you doing, like starving it! Since you don't care, then I don't care no more either! Fuck you and that baby!" he yelled as he casually walked away.

I was so hurt and angered by those things Sean had just said that I went ballistic and charged at his ass full force! I had caught him off guard, so he didn't even see that shit coming. I punched, kicked, scratched, and bit him. For the first time since we had been together, he fought me back. Well, he didn't punch me or nothing, but he did slap the shit out of me, twisted my arms behind my back, and pinned me down, refusing to let go until I calmed down. Once I saw that I couldn't break free of him and that shit started hurting, I broke down. I mean, I was crying so hard that my body started shaking uncontrollably. Any other time, Sean would have held me and assured me that everything was going to be okay, but not this time. He let me go and started throwing on clothes and grabbing his shit. I was stunned. This shit had never played out like this before.

As he walked past me to get his keys off his nightstand, I grabbed his leg and started begging, "Please don't go, Sean! Please! I'm sorry! I'll do anything you say. Just don't leave me alone again. I don't know what to do. I can't handle being by myself!"

He didn't utter a single word. Instead, he kicked me off his leg and kept it moving. I followed him, begging and pleading until he slammed the front door in my face! I was devastated, to say the least. I dragged myself back to my bed and called Shawni. She answered on the second ring. I told her everything and didn't spare any details. She knew I was having some issues behind what had happened because so was she, but she didn't know it was this bad. She assured me that he would come back and told me that I needed to give him some space. She also said it was probably as hard for him as it was for me to deal with what had happened to me. She said he was just angry and when he calmed down, he would be back. I told her that I hoped she was right, and that I'd talk to her later.

Just as I was removing the phone away from my ear, I heard her call my name. I put the phone back up to my ear without saying a word.

She said, "Sha Sha, are you there?"

I said, "Yes."

"I know it's hard, but you gotta find a way to block it out before it destroys you."

"I know, Shawni. I know."

"And you need to call Mama, Sha. She's starting to worry about you."

"You didn't tell her what happened, did you?"

"Girl no, you know I wouldn't do you like that. So just call her and act like everything is fine. She thinks that you don't want to have the baby, and that maybe Sean is forcing you."

"Oh."

"Well, is he Sha? Do you want it?"

"Yes, Shawni, I want my baby."

"Well you need to start acting like it and get it together!"

"I know, bye hooker!"

"Bye, Sasha!"

I crawled under the covers and went to sleep. Tomorrow was going to be a new day and a fresh start for me. I wasn't going to give up like the last time he left. I was going to pull it together for the sake of my unborn child and my man.

The next morning, I woke up at about 10:30 to an empty bed. I guess I hoped Sean would be there, snoring like he usually was but for some reason, I wasn't even sad or mad anymore. I knew what it took to make the situation right, and I was ready to do just that.

I had a doctor's appointment at 3:30 that I planned to attend, with or without Sean. I got up and threw on a pair of Sean's old sweats and a wife beater. I went into the kitchen, opened the refrigerator, and took out a bottle of Simply Orange orange juice along with a pear from the fruit drawer. I grabbed a glass from the cabinet and poured a half a glass of OJ. I drank my juice, took my pear with me into the living room, and took a seat on my white leather sectional with the purple piping. I had a big, round leather sofa table to match, with some end tables with glass tops on them. I had white leather lamps with the matching leather shades with purple piping. I also had a great big purple vase filled with purple, white, and black silk flowers.

My carpet was all white, from the living room to the dining room, which was decorated exactly the same. Under the living room and dining tables were big black mink rugs.

I grabbed the remote and hit the power button that turned on my 84-inch flat screen TV that was mounted on the adjacent wall. Judge Mathis' crazy ass was on, calling some dude a crackhead! That shit was so funny that I didn't even realize I was eating my pear until it was all gone. I guess that was the start because I didn't even feel sick afterward.

I picked up the cordless and called my interior decorator, Renee, and set up an appointment to have my walk-in closet turned into a nursery, and my empty bedroom downstairs turned into my closet and changing room. After that, I got up and did a little cleaning until it was time for me to get ready to go. I showered, flat ironed my hair, brushed my teeth, and got dressed; nothing fancy, just a pink Ed Hardy jogging suit with a black wife beater and some black and pink Ed Hardy Ugg-like boots. I slicked my hair over into a side ponytail, then put on my one-carat diamond studs and some of my Smashbox eyeliner and lip-gloss. Still no Sean, but I wasn't going to let that stop me or hold me back.

My visit was short and sweet. The doctor said that I had lost ten pounds since my last visit and to work on packing on some pounds, and no more sleeping pills. He gave me a prescription for some all-natural ones. I went home and forced down some chicken noodle soup, watched TV, played the Wii, and bullshitted on the Internet for the rest of the day. By 9:15, I was ready for bed.

I grabbed my iPhone and texted Sean the words, "I luv U, goodnight." By 9:30, I was out like a light. About 1:00 a.m., I got up to go pee and heard the living room TV on, which I was sure I had turned off. I walked into the living room to find Sean stretched out on the sofa watching ESPN.

I strolled over to him and grabbed his hand and whispered, "I'm sorry, baby. Come to bed." He quietly followed me into the room and climbed in bed behind me.

He held me close and whispered in my ear, "I'm sorry too, Sasha."

I placed his hand on my stomach and cried myself to sleep but this time, they were tears of joy.

For five months, things were running smoothly. After several dental appointments with one of the best dentists in the South, I had gotten a gold tooth implanted with a flawless diamond crown wrapped around it. My HIV test was negative, Shawni was running the shop, and I was having a baby girl! Sean had hired three security guards, and Shawni and Todd were a couple now, so he saw to it that she got home safely. I still came in once a week to make sure everything was running smoothly, but Sean wouldn't allow me to work, not until after the baby was born. My shop was one of the hottest shops in the ATL. I laid low, got fat, and finished decorating my home. The nursery was done, and it was beautiful! I had it decked out in all pink and khaki, from the crib sheets to the car seat to the stroller. She even had a pink wraparound couch and her own little bathroom, equipped with a child-sized toilet and sink. I had everything in order for our new arrival. Even though things had been rocky for the first couple of months, they had taken a turn for the better. Sean had been on his best behavior, for the most part. No bitches playing on my phone and he was coming in at a decent hour. He was being very attentive to all of my needs and hadn't missed a doctor's appointment since the time he had gotten mad and left.

Life was finally looking up for me. I couldn't believe that I was about to be somebody's mama! I had always wanted children but in my heart, I knew that me and Sean weren't mature enough to be nobody's parents. I didn't want my child to go through what I did as a child. With Sean running the streets all the time, anything could happen. I knew that we were still far from perfect but in a way, I felt like this baby was bringing us closer. It would slow us down, which was what we need anyway.

I had become a real homebody, only going out when I had to being that Sean did most of my running. It was a Saturday night, about 1:00 a.m., and Sean was out with his boys. I was just getting out of the tub after watching *I Can Do Bad All By Myself* when my cell phone rang. I wrapped the towel around my body, walked over to the nightstand, and picked it up. It was Shawni.

"Hello?"

"Hey Sha. What you doing?"

"Shit, just got out of the tub, about to get ready for bed. What's up?"

"Well, I got something to tell you, but I'm not going to tell you unless you can promise me that you won't trip."

"Is it about Sean?"

"Yeah, Sha. And don't start acting crazy when I tell you either."

"Shawni, I'm good."

"Okay, because the only reason I'm telling you this is to give you a heads up."

"Shawni, just tell me already! I'm cool, damn!"

"Well, I just left Ice, and guess who I seen Sean all bae'd up with?"

"Who?"

"Girl, that skank ass bitch that was claiming she was pregnant by him!"

"Bitch, you are lying!"

"I bullshit you not! They were all in the VIP popping champagne and shit."

"So, what did he do when he saw you?"

"He didn't see me because as soon as me and my girl Brealle came in, we headed straight for the bathroom. When we came out, I had Brealle cover me as we left right back out. It was him, Gutta,

Todd, her, her sister, and some other chick."

"Where you at now?"

"We are at my house. I'm waiting on Todd's punk ass to come home so I can check him."

"Oh, all right. Thanks for the heads up."

"Sha Sha, you sure you okay? Because you're a little too calm about this shit. You done flipped the script for shit way smaller than this."

"Girl, I'm so done with that bullshit. I've got bigger things to think about now, like this baby. I'm about to go to bed. I'll deal with that nigga in the morning."

"All right, Sha. I'll holla at you tomorrow."

"Good night, Shawni."

Unbeknownst to Shawni, my blood was boiling. I threw on some jeans, a t-shirt, and a pair of Air Max. I was so mad I didn't even bother to put on any underwear! I grabbed my purse, keys, Sean's two nines from underneath the mattress, and headed out the door. I jumped in the Lexus and was on my way to Club Ice! When I pulled into the parking lot, I drove around until I spotted Sean's car. I parked a couple of spaces over. I turned my car off and turned the radio up just as Trina's "Shawty Say" song came on. I sang along with the chorus.

"Shawty say the nigga that she wit ain't shit."

I reclined the seat until I was comfortable and waited for his exit. After about thirty minutes, it started to softly drizzle. I leaned forward and turned on the wipers so I wouldn't miss anything. Just as I was sitting back, out walked Sean and to my surprise, the bitch was walking with him! I jumped out the car with the two nines at my side and walked over to his truck.

When he saw me, he froze dead in his tracks. Once she saw what had stopped him, she stopped too, but with a smirk on her face. I didn't utter a word, but he did.

He told her that she should leave and she said, "But I don't have a ride. They already left."

"Look! I don't know what to tell you, so kick rocks!"

Just as she was about to turn and walk away, I raised the nines and pointed them at both of their heads. She was about to pop off until I walked up on her, then she froze dead in her tracks.

Without any warning, I turned around and unloaded both clips on Sean's Navigator, making sure I took out his windshield, headlights, and two front tires. People started scattering like roaches do when somebody turns on the lights!

I heard Sean yell, "Stupid, bitch!"

I was in such a trance that I didn't even realize that it had started pouring down raining. *Good*, I thought to myself, because I sure as hell didn't want to give them the satisfaction of seeing me cry.

I turned around with the guns raised and screamed, "Looks like both of yawl need a ride now!"

I quickly backed up to my still running car, aiming at them as I went until I reached the door handle. I got in and sped off toward home. When I got home, I stripped out of the wet clothes. I threw on another t-shirt and some panties and went to bed. Shockingly, I didn't even cry one time. I guess I was finally getting numb to this shit.

Sean didn't come home until 9:00 the next night. I was lying on the sofa watching an old episode of *The Bad Girls Club* that I had missed a couple of weeks before.

When he walked through the door and saw me, he stopped and started grilling me. He was freshly dressed in an all-black leather hooded jogging suit.

I spoke first. "Hi, honey. You're home," I said sarcastically.

"I'm glad you find this shit funny, Sasha."

"Naw nigga, it ain't hardly funny. It's fucked up! How you keep trying to play me, especially for some 'ole ratchet, lying ass, hoodrat bitch like her? A bitch who is so trifling she don't know who her bastard ass baby daddy is. So she tried to pin it on the highest bidder, which happened to be yo dumb ass!"

"Look Sasha, I'm sorry you had to see that shit, but it wasn't what you thought."

"Wow! Well, what would you call it then, Sean?"

"I was using her to get next to her brother and his people who raped you. Luckily, I had already got the hook up before you came out acting all wild west like Lisa Raye and Lil' Kim in that western they did."

"Bullshit! How the fuck you get her to roll on her own brother?"

"Girl, little do you know I've been tracking these niggas since that shit happened to you. What did you think I was going to do? Just let that shit ride? I used that stupid bitch to set up a meeting with her brother to buy some dope."

"So you mean to tell me he didn't know who you was?"

"Naw, he don't because she gave me the number and I did all the talking. He thinks my name is Rachad."

"Which is your middle name,"

"Now you got it!"

"Oh my God, Sean! I'm so sorry. I've fucked up your truck for nothing."

"Yeah, you did. But don't worry about it because you about to pay for it right now."

"What's that supposed to mean, Sean?"

It's like his anger returned when I said that. He yanked me up by my arm from the sofa and shoved the bag that he'd been holding the whole time into my hands and yelled, "Put it on!"

"What the fuck is wrong with you, Sean?"

"Just shut the fuck up and get dressed, Sasha! You think you so fucking gangster! Well, guess what soldier, it's time for you to earn your stripes for real. Now get dressed and let's go!"

I did as I was told and put on the jogging suit, which was identical to his, and the black Air Forces that were in there. He grabbed my hand and we headed out the door and hopped in a new all black Chevy Camaro that was parked in the driveway. Sean drove until we came up to an abandoned warehouse close to the projects in Bankhead. He pulled around back where there was a

Suburban and another car already parked. He parked and grabbed a black leather bag from the backseat and said, "Come on."

We got out and walked past the vehicles and into the warehouse. I spotted two men masked up with pistols pointed at the heads of two more men that were on their knees on the floor. It was two out of the three men who raped me. Instantly, I got short of breath and started to hyperventilate. Sean dropped the bag, then came up and hugged me from behind and whispered in my ear.

"It's okay baby, breathe. I'm right here. They can't hurt you anymore."

My breathing started to calm just from his touch alone, then he handed me some black leather gloves and helped me put them on my trembling hands. He put his on, then reached into the bag and pulled out two pistols with silencers already attached to them, handed one to me. I reluctantly took it as I made eye contact with him.

His piercing light brown eyes assured me that everything was going to be okay. He grabbed my hand and held it as we walked up to them, and then he let it go.

"Sasha baby, I know this is hard for you. But think about what the fuck they put you through and murk these mutherfuckers!"

I raised the gun to the nigga's head, which also happened to be the first one who shoved his nasty ass dick in my mouth. I closed my eyes and all I could see was Shawni's face the day they raped me. She looked just like I had as a child when I saw my daddy in that casket...terrified! I opened my eyes and in one swift motion, I aimed at his crotch and fired. I didn't even realize that the gun went off until I saw the agony in his face from trying to scream, which he couldn't do because his mouth was taped shut with a sock stuffed in it.

The crimson red blood was seeping from the front of his jeans. It felt good to see him suffer like I had when they raped me. I hoped he was feeling like less than a human being, just as I had that day. When I turned my head to see if Sean had approved of what I had done, I noticed that the other dude was lying on the ground lifeless with his eyes wide open.

That shit fueled my adrenaline, so I turned around and instructed Sean's goons to remove the first nigga's pants. Sean nodded his approval and they did it with no hesitation. What I saw made me gag. His penis was hanging halfway off! I aimed and fired, shooting the rest of that little mutherfucka off! I put the gun to his forehead and ripped the tape from his mouth, and dared him to scream. I removed the sock and threw it, then bent down and picked up his bleeding manhood. I stuffed it in his mouth–head first–and slid it in and out a couple of times before leaving it there!

I knelt down close to his ear and whispered, "Now that you know how it feels to suck a dick, you can burn in hell"!

As I stood up, I put the piece back to his forehead and watched him gag as I split his wig in two. Sean put his gun back in the bag and walked up behind me, slid the gun from my hands, and returned it to the bag as well. He then eased my gloves off and threw them in the bag, followed by his own gloves.

"Sasha, go get in the car."

I didn't answer. I just went and got into the car. I heard him tell his boys to clean that shit up, then I heard his footsteps coming up behind me. We got in the car and pulled off. I then heard an explosion. I looked in the rearview and saw flames and smoke, and the Suburban turning the corner. I laid back and closed my eyes. I had just taken a life, and remorse was now starting to set in. A single tear escaped my left eye and slid down my cheek. The entire ride home was eerily silent. As soon as we got in the house, I rushed into the bathroom and took a shower. I tried hard to scrub the scent of a dead man off my body.

When I was done, I dried off and put on my Betty Boop sleep shirt. Sean was already showered and in the bed. I climbed in and cuddled up so close to him that I could feel his heart beating.

He pulled the covers up on me, wrapped his strong arms around me and whispered, "I love you, Sasha. You did good. Now go to sleep and get some rest."

At that moment, I knew I would never leave Sean, no matter what he did. He was the only one in this world who made me feel safe and protected. At that moment, I loved him more than I loved myself, and I couldn't let him go. He was my air, and I knew I couldn't breathe without him. I think deep down in his heart, he knew it too.

YOU REAP WHAT YOU SOW

The next morning, I woke up in a cold sweat. I had had another nightmare. This time, I was being chased by the man whose life I had just taken. I was running toward a cliff and he was gaining on me. Just as the ground disappeared from up under my feet, I woke up. I tried to get up to go take a hot shower, but Sean's arms and leg were wrapped around me so tightly that I couldn't move. After prying him off of me, I got up and went into the kitchen and fixed him some French toast, scrambled eggs, and some turkey sausage links. I grabbed a breakfast tray and a glass, poured some orange juice into it, then placed it all on the tray and took it in to him.

"Sean, baby! Wake up! I made you breakfast!"

He didn't budge. I set the tray down on the nightstand, jumped on the bed, and started shaking him until he woke his butt up.

"Hey, baby! What's wrong?"

"Nothing. I made you some breakfast, so get up and eat it."

He leaned forward, kissed me firmly on the lips, and said, "Thank you."

I got the tray of food and set it over his lap, then headed to the shower to get dressed for the day; nothing fancy, just some maternity jeans and a white t-shirt. I put on some half-carat diamond studs, my platinum chain, with the three-carat "S" pendant. I put on some Victoria's Secret Cocoalicious lip gloss and my white and blue retros, then walked into the room just as Sean drank the rest of his orange juice.

"Baby, I'm leaving. You need anything while I'm out?"

"No, but my little friend here needs a little something before you go!"

"Boy bye, you and him are both nasty!"

"And you know you like us."

I kneeled down and whispered in his ear, "You wrong, Sean! I not only like the two of you, I love yawl!" then I grabbed my purse and keys and left. I just needed some me time to get my mind right.

The events from the night before and the dream were heavy on my mind, so I decided to go by the shop and shoot the shit with the girls for a minute, and then hit the spa for some much-needed pampering. When I got to the shop, it was jumping. I got a manicure, a pedicure, and an earful of much-needed gossip! I was glad that I came. I had forgotten how funny Shawni was until that day. She kept me laughing so hard I almost peed on myself twice! I didn't eat that morning, so I decided to go over to the restaurant and order me something.

"I'll be back. I'm going to get something to eat. Anybody want anything?"

Everybody said no, except Shawni's greedy butt.

"Order me some shrimp linguine, Sasha!"

"Alright. I'll be right back."

For some reason, I felt this eerie feeling wash over me. I brushed it off and said, "What up," to a couple of the dope boys chilling in front of the barbershop, and kept it moving.

I walked into the restaurant, up to the counter, and went to place my order when I heard a familiar voice say, "Look at this old high society bitch!"

I turned around and sure enough, it was Amaris. She was accompanied by another mud duck.

"Yeah, I'ma be a bitch! The bitch you wish you were every day of your miserable ass, I don't know who my baby daddy is life!"

"Oh, I know who my baby's daddy is."

I said, "Hhmph! Well, good for you."

I went to turn back around but before I could, she ran up and hit me with a hard right. Now, I was always taught by my older cousin NaNa that if you ever get jumped, grab the closest one and mop the floor with they ass and not to worry about the rest, so that's what I did! I grabbed her by her weave and started pounding on her face like I was Floyd Mayweather.

The other one was kicking me in the back and yelling, "Let my cousin go!"

I was in such a trance that I didn't feel anything. Everything was happening so fast that I didn't even feel William pulling me off of her until I saw her raise her foot up and kick me in my stomach. I kneeled down and clutched my stomach. The pain was so unbearable that I couldn't stand up. I looked around for anyone that could help when I saw Amaris and her cousin being thrown out the door by some of the guys who worked at the barbershop.

On her way out, she was hollering, "Payback's a bitch, ain't it? I hope you lose that baby!"

Someone yelled, "Call 911! She's bleeding!" I lay there, unable to move for what seemed like an eternity, until the ambulance came.

A couple of hours later, Kashmire Janay Caldwell, Kash for short, was brought into the world! She was breathtakingly beautiful! She was five pounds even and 17 inches long. She had peanut butter skin, big light brown eyes, and long, thick, jet black curly hair and eyebrows. She looked more like Sean than me, but she had my nose and lips.

That day was the happiest day of my life. I just sat there and stared at her as she fluttered her long, thick eyelashes like a butterfly for about five minutes. She was my freedom, my escape from all the drama and negativity, lies, and cheating. She was all I needed to get by. She was my little butterfly, my symbol of freedom. I no longer needed Sean to breathe. I never thought anyone could replace him, but she did. She was my breath of fresh air. I was laying there cradling her and waiting for Sean to come when my mom and Shawni walked in with a bouquet of white and red roses, the car seat, and the diaper bag.

"Hi, Mommy!"

"Ohh, give me my niece!"

"Dang, Shawni! What about me?"

"What about you? I can see that you okay, so you going to have to take a backseat now that she's here," Shawni said as she gently took my baby.

"Well, I still love you. How are you holding up?"

I said, "I'm fine, Mommy. Just very sore," as I cut my eyes at Shawni.

"Ma, come look at her. She is so pretty. What's her name, Sha Sha?"

"Kashmire Janay."

"So I take it Kash for short."

"I like it, Sasha!"

"Thank you, Mama." We passed Kash around and chit-chatted for the next thirty minutes, until Sean walked in.

"What's up Shawni, Mama?"

"Waiting on you, where have you been?" said my mom.

"I was way on the other side of town taking care of some business and had left my phone in the car. As soon as I got the message, I flew up here, Ma."

"Okay, boy! Now come on over here and see your daughter!"

Sean walked over and picked her up, then came, gave me a kiss and sat down on the bed next to me.

"Wow, Sash! She is so pretty, and she looks so much like me it's scary."

"I know. Don't she, baby?"

"Well, we gonna get up out of here and let ya'll do some bonding.

Come on, Shawni. Let's go."

"Alright ma. Sasha, I'll call you later. See you later Sean."

"Bye."

Sean stayed for the remainder of the day and all night with the baby so I could rest. The next morning, I was still sore. The nurse had to help me with a shower again. Meanwhile, Sean dressed and fed the baby. By 11:00 a.m., I was discharged and we were headed home with our little bundle of joy. Even though she was premature, she weighed enough to go home. If I would have gone full term, she would have been a little butterball!

When we got home, all I wanted to do was take a long, hot bath and eat something hearty. As I lay back in the tub and let the jets massage my aching body, I wondered if this was a sign from God. Were the events of yesterday payback from God for me taking that man's life? Then I thought aloud, "Probably not" because if it was, then my sweet baby wouldn't have made it.

When I came out of the bathroom, I didn't see Sean or Kash. I crept over to the door of her bedroom and saw something so beautiful. Sean was laid out on her couch, on his back with his shirt off asleep. Kash was lying on his chest with nothing but a diaper on, knocked out.

I grabbed my cell phone and took a picture of them. Maybe we would be good parents after all. I grabbed a throw that I had decorating the back of the couch and gently covered them up.

I went into the kitchen, found the phone book, and ordered two extra-large meat lover's pizzas, one with pineapple, and some buffalo wings.

Thirty minutes later, the doorbell rang. I sat my Vibe magazine down and went to answer the door.

Ding-dong ding-dong.

I grabbed my purse and went to pay for the pizza. By the time I came back into the room with the food, Sean was lying on the bed flipping through the channels with Kash sitting in her car seat. Her eyes were wide open, watching TV as well.

"I guess there's a new queen of this castle now, huh?"

"Naw, baby! You still the queen bee and she's the princess. Now come over here and give me a slice of that pizza!"

The next two weeks were wonderful! I loved being a mommy, and I was pretty sure Sean was loving being a dad. He was so attentive to all of her needs. You would have thought he birthed her himself. Life was looking up for us finally.

It was the third week that was hell, though. I awoke one morning to Kash screaming at the top of her lungs. I crawled out of bed, leaving Sean sound asleep, and went into the kitchen to fix her a bottle. When I went into her room and picked her up, she was drenched in sweat. I picked her up, took off her nightgown, and walked into the bathroom to run her some water. I fed her and she calmed down, but was still a little cranky, then I bathed her and washed her hair and dressed her.

I sat down on her sofa and gently rocked her back to sleep. As soon as I thought she was fully sleep, I got up and tried to lay her back in her crib. As soon as her head hit the pillow, she started crying again. I picked her back up and began rocking her again. She wouldn't stop for nothing. I walked her, patted her, rocked her, and sang to her for the next hour, but nothing seemed to be working. I figured she must have colic.

I lay on the sofa with her on my chest, crying with my eyes closed while she cried. I didn't know what else to do. I guess I wasn't cut out to be a mother after all. I felt helpless. How could I not know what was wrong with my own baby? I opened my eyes when I felt Sean take Kash off my chest, and then sit down next to me.

"What's wrong, Sash?"

I felt so bad. All I could do was ball up and cry. Sean got up, put her in her swing, and started it up. As soon as that swing started, she stopped crying. I felt even worse because that was the one thing I hadn't tried. Sean came back over to me, picked me up, and carried me into the bedroom. He lay me down on the bed, then went into the bathroom, got a warm washcloth, and washed my tears away. Afterward, he sat down in front of me.

"Sasha, it's okay to get overwhelmed, you know?"

I didn't answer.

"You know, Ma, you've been doing a great job with her and at times, she's going to stress you out, but that's what I'm here for. So when you're feeling like you're at your breaking point, that's where I come in. Okay?"

I nodded yes. He kissed me on my forehead and said, "Now, get up and get dressed. I got a surprise for you. And put on something sexy while I go check on Kash and get her ready to go."

"I love you, Sean."

"I know. And I love you, too, babe."

I thought back to the day Kash was born and the fight that brought her here so early. Me and Sean never discussed the incident at all. For some reason, he never asked me what happened, maybe because they had already told him at the restaurant, or maybe we never brought it up because we were just so happy to have Kash here that it was irrelevant. Either way, it didn't matter because it brought me and Sean closer together, gave us something worth more than any material possession that we had—or should I say somebody!

I got up and picked out something to wear. I opted for a black fitted, one-shoulder Gucci dress that enhanced my cleavage with the crystal belt that had the logo on it. I grabbed the matching strappy crystal four-inch stilettos with the big double G closure. To accent my outfit, I'd wear simple diamond earrings and matching necklace and bracelet.

I bathed and flat ironed my hair bone straight with a swoop flipped back and a red rose stuck in the other side. I put on my clothes, shoes, and jewels, and felt like Sister in the favorite movie, *Sparkle*. I was loving my new figure. I had lost all of my added weight, except for about ten pounds, which all seemed to have gone to my ass.

After I finished admiring my new body and applying some M.A.C. eyeliner, mascara and peach lip-gloss, I went to check on my two babies. I was feeling just like one of MJB's songs, "So Lady."

When I went into the bedroom, Kash was sitting in her car

seat. She looked so cute wearing a gray and black signature Gucci dress with a matching bonnet that her curly bangs crept out from under, some black leggings, and matching Gucci boots. He walked out of his bathroom and stopped dead in his tracks when he saw me.

"Damn baby, you make me want to say fuck going out, and bend you right over that bed and try for making a baby brother for Kash!"

I couldn't do anything but blush. He was looking damn good himself in his black Gucci jeans and crisp grey Gucci long-sleeved button-down, and his signature grey and black Gucci loafers. I think he had more Gucci in his closet than any store in the city! He loved that shit like Michael did that mouse in the Jackson Five movie!

"I know ya'll didn't just accidentally end up wearing the same thing as me!"

"Naw, baby! I looked at your outfit while you were in the shower."

"Oh."

"I already got the baby's diaper bag packed, so grab her blankets, your jacket, and let's go."

When we got outside, there was a stretch 2010 Cadillac limo truck parked in the driveway. There was a tall white gentleman wearing a black tuxedo standing next to the limo. He held the door open for us. I got in first and took the car seat from, Sean then slid over for him to get in. There was a fully stocked bar, mirrored ceilings, a sink, a mini fridge, and a snack bar.

I rolled the window down so I could take in the fresh air. This was the first time I had been out since I had Kash and I must admit, it felt good.

Sean had even taken her to her first doctor's appointment, saying that I needed to rest.

Before I knew it, we had pulled up to a professional portrait studio and for the next two hours we took several family portraits; then, Sean told me that we were taking the baby over to Shawni's for her and Todd to watch.

"What? Boy, are you crazy? They can barely even take care of themselves!"

"Girl, shut up! Kash will be fine. They've been asking to keep her for a minute. They say they're thinking about having one of their own. I guess, they are too immature for kids."

After we dropped Kash off at Shawni's condo, we headed to one of my favorite restaurants, The Cheesecake Factory. Dinner was going swell, and then it was time for some dessert. I was looking over the cheesecake menu when Sean excused himself to go to the restroom. I had just placed our orders for a slice of turtle cheesecake for Sean, which happened to be his favorite, and a slice of cherry cheesecake, my favorite, when he returned to the table. He had a huge smile plastered on his face.

"What are you cheesing so hard for?" I asked him.

"Nothing, just admiring how beautiful you are."

My heart almost melted. He reminded me so much of the Sean

that I had met years ago.

As soon as I opened my mouth to speak, the waiter walked up with our desserts and we thanked him. I started digging into mine right away while Sean sat staring at me like I was his entertainment. I just giggled and took another bite as he got up, came around the table, and knelt down on one knee.

I opened my mouth to ask him what he was doing when I almost choked on some foreign object in my dessert. I pulled it out and started screaming! Once I calmed down, Sean took the ring, then placed it on my finger and popped the question!

"Sasha, will you marry me?"

"Yes! Yes! Yes! I will! Oh my God, yes!

We stood up and kissed. I kissed him so passionately that you would have thought we were in the privacy of our own bedroom. Everybody stood up and cheered, and a few people came over and said congratulations. We gathered our things and left. I was so ecstatic that I couldn't stop staring at my ring. It was a flawless five-carat heart-shaped, pink diamond ring set in platinum.

The next stop kind of threw me off. It was an upscale tattoo boutique, as they called it. I just followed suit without saying a word. Once we got inside, we were greeted by the receptionist. Sean spoke up and said that we had an appointment, and gave her his name. She looked it up and then we were escorted to the back.

The tattoo artist asked him what he wanted, and Sean simply said, "Her."

I was so taken aback by his answer that I just stood there speechless until the guy pulled up a chair and asked me to sit in it, and be as still as possible. I obliged. Sean took his shirt off and laid flat on his back on top of the table, and the artist went to work. It took him three and a half hours to create this masterpiece, and I was so anxious to see it that as soon as the tattoo gun stopped, I jumped up to get a look at it!

"Wow, Sean! It looks so life-like!"

It looked exactly like me from the neck up—earrings, necklace, rose in my hair and all! It covered his whole chest and half of his stomach. He got up and walked over to the mirror to get a look at it.

"Damn, baby! It does look exactly like you!"

At that moment, in spite of all the negative things people may have said about our relationship and Sean's infidelity, I knew that deep down that he really did have unconditional love for me.

Sean put his shirt back on and paid the man his fee of $400.00, plus a $100 tip. Once we got back into the limo, Sean suggested that we go to a bar and have a couple of drinks, and I agreed. We found a nice little bar downtown and were on our third round of Patrón with pineapple juice. We were really enjoying our date night. I was a little taken aback when Sean ordered the first round though, because he never drank liquor; champagne every now and then, but never liquor. I guess that night was special, though. We were now engaged.

For the next 30 minutes, we laughed, drank, danced, and we

reminisced about all the good times we had shared, then my phone rang.

"Hello?"

"Sha, you need to get here now. Something is wrong with Kash!" she said frantically.

"What? What do you mean, Shawni? Calm down! What's wrong with my baby?"

"I don't know. She's coughing up blood and won't stop crying. I called an ambulance, so just meet us at the hospital by my house."

I dropped the phone in shock. Sean's grabbing my arm and shaking me brought me back into reality.

"Sasha, what's wrong, baby?"

"It's Kash! Something's wrong with her. We got to get to the hospital now."

Sean paid our tab and we jumped in the limo, headed to the hospital.

GOD COULDN'T BE THIS CRUEL

As soon as we stepped into the emergency room, Shawni and Todd ran up to us.

"Where's Kash, Shawni?"

"They rushed her straight back. I don't know what's going on with her yet."

I pushed her out of my way and rushed up to the nurse's station with Sean right behind me. I was greeted by one of the nurses.

"Hi! How may I help you?"

"My name is Sasha Parham, and our baby was just brought in and rushed to the back. I need to find out what was going on with her."

"What's her name?"

"Kashmire Caldwell."

"Okay. Give me a few minutes and I'll be right back with some information for you."

"Alright. Thank you."

Sean and I stood in the same spot for what seemed like forever when the nurse came back out with the doctor, who just so happened to be the same one who treated me after the rape.

He walked up to us and said, "I'm sorry, Mr. & Mrs. Caldwell, but Kashmire didn't make it."

I yelled, "What the fuck do you mean, she didn't make it? What the fuck happened? She was fine a couple of hours ago!"

"I'm sorry ma'am, but she had a tiny hole in one of her lungs, which caused it to gradually fill with blood, which is why she was coughing up blood. She also had some internal bleeding that we could not stop."

"I don't believe you! I want to see my baby now!"

"Right this way, ma'am. And again, I'm truly sorry for your loss, but there was nothing that we could do. I am very surprised that she fought this long. This is something that they should have caught at birth."

As we walked, I tuned out everything he said because I was not going to believe she was gone until I saw it for myself. Once we reached the room, Sean and I were the only ones allowed to go in. We were led over to a table where the doctor pulled back a tiny white sheet on a gurney.

She looked so peaceful, as if she was just asleep. I walked up to her, knelt down and kissed her lips. I started whispering, "Kash baby, please wake up!" then the tears started rolling. I guess it had finally started to sink in that it was true…that she was really dead. My whispers turned into begging screams as Sean dragged me out of the room kicking and screaming.

"Don't go! Don't go! Mommy needs you! I won't make it without you here!"

Sean carried me all the way back to the limo and forced me inside. Once we were inside, he cradled me in his lap and held me tightly as we cried together. I must have cried myself to sleep because when I opened my eyes, we were at home. Sean opened the door and got out to go open the front door. When he returned, he tipped the driver three $100 bills, and then came and helped me out of the car and into the house. I showered, put on some boy shorts with a matching baby tee, grabbed a blanket from the hall closet, and went into Kash's room. I locked the door, curled up on her couch, and went to sleep. I woke up the next morning, used the bathroom, and laid back down. Sean must have heard me moving around because he came to the door and asked if I was okay.

"I'm fine, Sean. I just want to be left alone."

"All right, baby. When you feel better, call your mom. She's worried about you."

"Okay."

For the next two days, I refused to leave her room. I just wanted to be near her, to smell her. I wanted to stay here forever. I wanted her to come back. No, I needed her to come back, but I knew that was not going to happen, so I took what I could get. My mother had been by twice, along with Shawni, KeKe, and some of his family members. Sean assured them that I was fine and just needed some time alone. I guess they understood because they left without a hassle.

On the third night, I decided to come out. I guess that I had punished Sean enough. At first, I blamed him for her death because if he hadn't fucked that silly ho, none of this would've happened. I couldn't stand to look at him. After some rational thinking, I realized that I was wrong, and that he was probably hurting just as bad as I was. I mean, it's not like he knew that something like this would happen.

When I came out, Sean was laying in the bed watching Law and Order: SVU, which was my favorite show. He was eating some Jets barbeque chicken pizza. I climbed into the bed, grabbed a slice, and started watching TV. Sean was the first to break the ice.

"Baby, you know we have to start making funeral arrangements."

"Sean, I know this may sound selfish, but I can't. I'm just not strong enough."

"You can do it, Ma. Don't worry. You'll be fine."

"No Sean, I won't. You, Shawni, my mom, and your parents can do it."

"Whatever you want bae, I got you. I'll take care of everything."

Her funeral was two days later. I heard it was very nice. I didn't attend. I just refused to let her go. I just couldn't bear the closing of the casket. I went and sat with her and read to her. I told her how much I loved her at the wake the same day. I didn't let anybody know that there was going to be a wake because that would be me and Sean's time alone with her right before the funeral. They had dressed her and done her hair perfectly. She was breathtaking.

Sean had gotten her a satin cream-colored dress with bell sleeves and a big bow at the waist, with a matching headband with the same bow on it. He bought her the cutest cream socks with lace and little bows on them. She looked so heavenly that I knew she would fit right in with the rest of the angels up there.

I left Sean at the church right before the funeral was to start and went to pick up the 100 rare butterflies I had special ordered. After I picked them up, I went to the cemetery where she was going to be buried and let them free. I said a special prayer for her and blew a kiss into the sky. Just as I turned to leave, the hearse was pulling into the cemetery. I slipped my Chloe shades down over my eyes and quickly walked to my car. I headed home, wondering what the rest of my future held.

When I got home, the first thing I did was slip off my Giuseppes and Dolce and Gabbana skirt set. I didn't even bother to bathe. I took a valium to calm my nerves, got in the bed, and went to sleep. For the next couple of weeks, I stayed cooped up in the house depressed. I wouldn't recognize sunlight if I saw it. Sean seemed to hit the streets even harder. It was as if that was the only way he knew how to cope with our loss.

I was chilling one night, watching "Tiny and Toya" when Sean walked in after being gone all day. Being that we didn't talk much lately, what he said threw me off a little.

"Sasha, go pack our toiletries, iPods, and underwear, and then go get some sleep. We've got an early flight."

"Nigga, don't just come up in here giving out orders when I've barely seen or talked to you in the last few days!"

"I know, baby. I know. I've been real distant lately, but I couldn't just sit here and watch you suffering like this. I mean, look at you. You're losing weight, you haven't combed your hair in weeks. You barely wash your ass and you're sleeping all day." I couldn't even respond because he was right.

"Sash, enough is enough. I called myself giving you some time to clear your head, but I see that ain't working. If I don't step in now, you'll sit here and deteriorate. So get up and do as I said because we're going to Hawaii in the morning, whether you want to or not. And believe me, I will drag your ass out of here kicking and screaming."

Shit! He wouldn't have to drag me. I was game as soon as I heard him say Hawaii!

ALOHA

It all seemed so surreal. To think, just the night before, I could hardly sleep. The anticipation was killing me! Now, I was stepping off of a plane and into the sunset with my boo. The scenery was something hood chicks like me only dreamed about.

"Baby! Baby! Look at the trees and the pretty tropical flowers! Aren't they beautiful?"

"Yeah Sasha, but you haven't seen nothing yet. Wait until you see the hotel we're going to be staying in for the next week."

"Thank you, Sean. I really needed this vacation."

"Girl, I love you and whatever you want or need, you shall receive."

We checked into our $1,500 a night penthouse suite in Kauai and spent the rest of the day shopping on their version of Rodeo Drive. I had a blast spending Sean's money and dining at one of the best seafood restaurants the island had to offer. By the time we made it back, I was exhausted. I got undressed and slid into the hot tub with nothing but my hot pink thong on.

"Hey Sean, why don't you come and join me?"

"You sure, because you know if I come and get in, I'm gonna wanna fuck."

"I'm positive. Mama's been missing daddy lately."

Sean got butt naked and stepped into the tub. I stepped out of my thong and sat on his lap as he slid his pulsating manhood into my throbbing, hot vagina. I gasped as he entered me and started

117

riding him like I was a cowgirl riding a bucking bronco. We were both so backed up that we both climaxed back to back within five minutes.

"Oh, baby! I really needed that," I said as I tried to catch my breath.

"I know you did, baby. And it was my pleasure to help you release. Let's dry off so you can get some sleep. I've got a big day planned for you tomorrow."

We got out and dried each other off, then got under the 600 thread count Egyptian cotton sheets and fluffy sparkling white comforter and cuddled until we fell fast asleep, wrapped in each other's arms. I was awakened the next morning by the sun peeking through the drapes that we left slightly cracked last night. Sean was standing in the front of the huge bay window watching the sun rise. When he heard me yawning, he quickly turned around startled, as if he had momentarily forgotten that I was in the room.

"Hey babe! I'm glad you finally woke up."

"What time is it, honey?"

"Girl, it's 7:00 a.m."

"Boy, you talking about finally woke up? Shit, it's still considered night time in my book!"

"I'm sorry, baby. I'm just so excited, I couldn't sleep. I didn't mean to wake you. Psych!!! Get up and throw on your bikini and let's go for a swim. It's not every day that we go to wake up in Hawaii!"

I reluctantly dragged myself out of the bed and into the

shower. Sean joined me and we washed each other quickly, then retreated back to the room and put on our swimwear. I was rocking a hot orange terrycloth Juicy Couture bikini with matching flip flops. Sean was wearing a pair of board shorts and a pair of flip flops. We grabbed our towels and hit the door. Shockingly, we weren't the only two idiots on the beach this early. I grabbed Sean by the hand and we ran into the big blue ocean like two teenagers in love. I didn't have a care in the world at the moment. I was in love, and it felt good. For the first time since Kash died, I was happy. It was as if she was giving me permission to live again after her death. She brought me so much joy in her short life. Maybe she was just a messenger of God, sent here to show us that there was more to life than material things, selling drugs, and being one of the flyest couples in Atlanta. She taught us how to love. It was like she was an epiphany.

Sean snapped me out of my trance by picking me up and throwing me into the water. We spent the rest of the morning frolicking around on the beach. At about noon, Sean told me that he had a spa day full of pampering set up for me. We found our shoes and headed to the designated spa area of the hotel. Sean headed back to the room, and I was escorted to a dressing room and was instructed by the masseuse to shower and slip into the silk robe. I did as I was told, and wrapped my hair up in a plush head wrap. When I came out of the dressing room, she greeted me and led me to a massage table. I was treated to a facial, French manicure, and pedicure.

Next, I was taken to the hotel salon and had my hair washed, straightened, and barrel curled. They waxed my eyebrows and did my makeup, and then finished it off with a Brazilian wax. When I was done, I gathered my things and headed back up to the penthouse. I was greeted by two women holding a sign with my name on it when I stepped off the elevator.

"Hi. Can I help you, ladies?"

"No, ma'am. We're here to help you get dressed for the evening."

"Excuse me, but help me what?"

In unison, they both said, "To help you get dressed for this evening's festivities. Now follow us, please."

I followed them to the living area where there were a dozen shopping bags from Harry Winston, Saks, and Dolce and Gabbana.

"What is Sean up to?" I asked out loud to no one in particular. The women giggled discreetly.

"What's so funny?"

"Nothing," they said quickly as they started pulling things out of the bags.

One of them handed me a beautiful chiffon soft yellow Dolce and Gabbana halter gown with a low plunge in the back, which stopped right above my butt. In the front, it was fully embellished from the waist up. They helped me put it on. It was so long that it cascaded around me.

Next, one of them slipped a pair of five-carat pink diamond chandelier earrings into my ears while the other put on the matching bracelet. I was so overwhelmed that I had to sit down. As soon as I sat down, one of them picked up my foot and slid a platinum toe ring onto it while the other one curled my hair and put a platinum tiara on top of it. They grabbed my hands and pulled me to the full-length mirror. As soon as I saw myself, I gasped.

"Wow! I look like a princess."

"You sure do, ma'am. Now come on, your prince is waiting."

Both of them locked arms with me and proceeded to escort me out of the room. They led me down to the first level to a set of closed doors. One of them opened the doors, and my mouth and heart dropped at the same time. There were about two rows of white chairs holding my mom, Chuck and his girlfriend, my friend KeKe, my cousin NaNa, Sean's mom, his dad, and his grandma. Soft yellow, purple, and lavender flowers were draped everywhere. White and yellow rose petals adorned the sand in between the chairs, creating a path to the altar where Ashawni and Todd were standing on either side. Sean and the pastor were standing in the middle. The sun was just starting to set. Ashawni was wearing a short silky lavender wrap dress with a yellow flower pinned in her hair. Sean had on a crisp, all-white short-sleeved Gucci button up with some crisp white, yellow, and purple plaid shorts. Todd had on the same outfit, except his shorts didn't have the purple in them. He was the spitting image of Sean, except two shades darker and wore bald head. Everyone was barefoot, just like me.

As I started to walk, I heard a very familiar voice singing Mary J's "Everything." I started to look around and found the face that matched the voice. I turned to my left, and there she was, in an all-white, floor-length strapless dress with a lily pinned on the side of her short feathered hairstyle. She was holding a gold mic and serenading me. I thought I was dreaming! It was Mary J. Blige herself!

Instantly, tears flooded my vision. Somehow, I made it to the altar. The ceremony was about 15 minutes long. Afterward, I got to see Mary, and she was so down to earth and humble. She took pictures with me, Sean, and all of our family and friends. The ballroom was beautifully decorated with all white crystal chandeliers, ribbons, and crystal vases trimmed in gold and filled with different color tropical flowers.

I escorted Mary, Kendu, and the rest of her entourage to the feast. There was fried chicken, lobster, garlic shrimp, broiled scallops with bacon, and steamed vegetables. They ate while Sean and I had our first dance to Keyshia Cole's "Sent from Heaven."

For there not to be a big guest list, the place was packed because Sean had invited everyone working and staying at the hotel to the reception to show his gratitude for helping him make this day special. I later found Shawni walking around admiring my fresh bouquet of white lilies that she had caught after the ceremony. It was so funny to see her with it that I let out a slight chuckle.

It was funny because when I reached the altar and she handed it to me, she whispered, "Bitch, you betta toss it to me!"

I did; poor Todd!

The sun was setting, but the night was still young. The DJ was playing "Sex Room" by Ludacris, and just as I was coming up to Shawni, Todd grabbed her hand and they headed to the dance floor. I turned around to look for Sean, but he was gone too. I walked around the entire room, and still no Sean. I headed outside and sure enough, there he was.

As soon as I opened my mouth to speak, he started cussing someone out. His back was to me, so he didn't even notice me walking up behind him. As I got closer, I stopped. He was on his Blackberry. I stood there and listened.

He was saying, "Bitch, what is wrong with you? You a silly ass broad, you know that? It's just sex, nothing more! Bitch, I got a wife! What part don't you get? I'm trying to enjoy my fucking wedding reception, so don't call me back again! As a matter of fact, lose my number!"

I couldn't believe this nigga was talking to one of his hoes at our wedding reception! I walked right past him as he ended the conversation and headed to the beach. I heard him whisper, "Damn!"

I sat down on the sand at the edge of the water and let the ocean wash away my tears. Sean came up behind me, removed his Polo flip flops, and sat down beside me. We sat in silence and listened to the waves.

After about ten minutes he said, "Sasha, I'm sorry. I'm trying, but I just can't seem to get this faithful shit right."

"Sean, what's wrong with me? Why can't I be enough? I cook,

I clean, I suck your dick at the drop of a dime. What is it? Am I not pretty enough?"

"Baby, it's not you. It's me. I love you, but I like the excitement of conquering new pussy also. I wasn't always like this. I guess when you got locked up, that's how I dealt with the loneliness and now I can't seem to shake the habit."

"So why marry me, Sean? Why even wait for me? You could have moved on. I could have moved on. Why make us suffer?"

He wrapped his arms around me and held me tightly. I could feel his tears on my neck.

"Because I love you girl, and I can't and won't ever let you go. I will kill you before I see you with anyone else but me. Don't you understand? We are soulmates. Yeah, I'm going to fuck other bitches, but the only one I will ever love, give my children to, give my last name or heart to is you. I will die and kill for you. woman! So bear with me, baby. I promise you from this day forward I will do better."

He kissed me and slid his tongue into my mouth, and intertwined it with mine.

Sean must have requested that the DJ play all of my favorite songs because that couldn't have just been a coincidence. After that, it was Trey Songz, "Jupiter Love." I grabbed Sean's belt, unfastened it, and gently caressed his manhood. It stood at attention and welcomed the warmth of my left hand and the cold platinum of my three-carat wedding band and five-carat engagement ring. He pulled me onto his lap and raised my dress.

He slid my underwear to the side underneath my wedding dress. Right then and there, on the beach, we consummated our union and became one, infidelity and all.

BACK TO THE HOOD OF THINGS

It was a Friday, and I was sitting in the living room reading a new Terri McMillan novel. I was so bored. All of my girls were busy, and Shawni was working at the shop, so I decided to call Sean. I hit him up on speed dial, and the phone rang about five times before a female answered. I removed the phone from my ear and looked at it, thinking that I must have dialed the wrong number.

Nope, I sure didn't! When I put my phone back to my ear, all I heard was, "Look, bitch! Sean is sleep. Call him back later," from the female on the other end.

I was so mad, I could have sworn I was breathing fire! I kept my cool and refrained from getting indignant.

I calmly said, "Well, when he wakes up, tell him to call his wife."

The chick said, "Yeah, whatever," then I heard was a dial tone.

Now I knew I was maturing because I was still sitting there about to finish reading my book!

An hour later, Sean came walking through the door looking all paranoid and shit. I just played it cool and didn't even bring it up. Instead, I asked him if he wanted to grab some movies and take out.

"No babe, I've got some moves to make and money to pick up."

"Well, what about when you're done?"

"Oh, me and Todd are supposed to meet up at the strip club."

"Oh, okay."

"Won't you and Shawni go and hang out?"

"Shawni's at…I mean, I don't have anything to wear."

"Here," he said as he pulled a knot out of his pocket and handed it to me. He started heading for the kitchen.

"Hey Sean, why didn't you answer when I called you a little while ago?"

"Oh uh, my phone was in the car and by the time I realized you called, I was on my way home anyway."

"Oh, okay."

This nigga must have been high on crack, trying to play me for stupid! That's why I taxed his ass every chance I got. Why spend my chips when I could spend his? He knew it too, but guilt is a trip, ain't it?

If he thought that shit was over, then he was dumb as fuck! I grabbed my keys and hit the door. First stop, the salon.

Later on that night…

It was 1:00 a.m., and I was nervous as hell! Psych! I was amped! I peeked out past the stage to see if I saw Sean. Yup, there him and his boys were, front row center. Ciara's "Like a Boy" started blasting form the speaker as the DJ announced the first act as Ecstasy for amateur night. I crawled onto the stage wearing a red see-through lace La Pearla boy short and bra set with a red and blue Atlanta baseball fitted, and some six-inch red knee-high stiletto boots. I crawled over to the pole and inched my way to the top. Once there, I flipped into an upside-down split. I slid down just like that and my hat flipped off, revealing my newly dyed honey blonde locks of hair. I came down slowly and landed on my neck and the back of my head in that upside-down split.

The niggas went crazy, throwing money like it literally grew on trees. I got up and started working the stage, showing out like I do. When I got right in front of Sean, I started unsnapping my bra while I ground to the beat. Our eyes locked after his roamed all over my body, and he threw five Benjamin's at my feet. Suddenly he realized it was me. He grabbed me off the stage, threw me over his shoulder, and headed for the exit while niggas continued to throw money at me. I smiled a devilish smile and gave myself a standing ovation in my mind.

We rode home in silence. When we got in the house, I headed straight for the tub until Sean grabbed my arm and swung me around.

"Come here, Sasha—oops, I mean Ecstasy! Since you want to go all player's club on a nigga, go on downstairs and give me a private dance!"

"Okay."

He followed me downstairs and turned on the sound system. "Skin" by R. Kelly came on. I put on a show for my husband until I was fully nude, except for my boots, and the song went off. Sean got up, grabbed a bottle of Moët from the bar, and popped it open.

"Here, Sasha. You look hot!"

I grabbed the bottle and took a sip; my throat was very dry from the coke I had sniffed at the club. I started to walk off the stage when Sean grabbed me by the hair, threw me down next to the pole, and started yelling.

"Get back up there, hoe! You ain't finished until I say you're finished!"

"Fuck is wrong with you, nigga?"

"You wanna shake ass for some niggas you don't know, but not for me? Huh?"

He grabbed the bottle of Moët from my hands and started pouring it on me while he kicked and verbally degraded me. I just laid there in shock until my survival instincts kicked in, then I started kicking his crazy ass wildly with my heels. We fought for about ten minutes until I was too exhausted to continue and fight him back, yet he continued to hit me like I was a nigga in the street. After another couple of painful minutes, he stopped. He leaned over me and asked me why as the tears slid down his cheeks.

"Why do you want to make me this angry, Sasha? Why make me hurt you like this when all I want to do is to protect and love you?"

"Because you crossed the line letting that bitch answer your phone. I don't even have the nerve to answer your phone!"

"Damn baby, all over some silly bitch! I'm sorry, but that is not an excuse for your slutty behavior."

He got up and headed up the stairs. I hated him at that moment. I couldn't stand to be near him, so I got up and went upstairs and slept in the guest room. My life and my marriage were dying, and I didn't know how to revive it.

The next morning, I awoke with a banging headache. My body was so sore I could barely move. The only place he hadn't hit or kicked me was in my face. I don't know what happened to him. Before I got locked up, he would never put his hands on me. He was the sweetest, gentlest giant you would ever meet. I would have never imagined that I would be in an abusive relationship, but here I was!

I got up and went into the connecting bathroom and started running some bath water. I stripped off my boots and climbed in. I laid back and relaxed. I had some soul searching to do. Maybe I had changed also. I mean, five years was a long time. The world has changed a lot too since then.

Maybe prison had hardened my heart because in the past, I never would have provoked Sean the way that I do, and I was pretty sure that the streets had hardened him also.

The sudden loss of our daughter could play a part in our erratic behavior also. Maybe we were still grieving. Maybe we needed to seek some therapy.

An hour later, I grabbed a towel off the bar behind me and got out of the tub. I didn't even bother drying off. I just wrapped it around me and headed downstairs in search of some Aleve. I found some in my purse on the kitchen cabinet. I grabbed some orange juice from out of the refrigerator and poured a glass. After I took the pill and gulped down my juice, I headed to my dressing room for something to wear. I settled on a pair of skinny jeans, a white MK tee, and some white corked wedges. I went to our bedroom and into my bathroom, grabbed a black bra and thong, and got dressed.

Sean was still snoring, thank God. I was not ready to face him yet. I didn't even bother to apply any makeup. I just pulled my hair up into a raggedy ponytail with a white headband and applied some lip gloss. I grabbed my brown Gucci swingback and checked the mirror to make sure my VVS stones were still in my ears. I was relieved when I saw them both still glistening.

Once I located my keys and phone, I was out. First stop, the hair store in Bankhead. I bought a black hooded jogging suit and a black skull cap–and yes, they do sell that shit at the hair stores in the hood!

Next, I hit the mall and bought a pair of all-black Nikes and some black Nike socks from Finish Line. I was now ready to do a caper!

Just as I was leaving, my phone rang. It was a private number, so I started to let it go but something told me I should answer, so I did.

"Hello?"

"What's up, sexy?"

"Nothing, who is this?"

"This is Malik."

For some strange reason, my heart skipped a beat.

"How did you get my number, Malik?"

"Your sister gave it to me at the Waffle House this morning. Is it a problem?"

"No. Just wondering," I said as I made a mental not to kick Shawni in her big ass!

"So, I was wondering if we could do lunch, for old time's sake?"

My mind said no, but my mouth beat it to the punch.

"Sure. Just name the place and I'll meet you there."

"Meet me at The Cheesecake Factory in 30!"

"Okay. Bye, Malik."

"Goodbye, sexy."

I blushed as I hung up the phone. I got to the restaurant about 35 minutes later. I tore up all of my receipts and dropped them in the trashcan on my way in.

Malik was already seated, so I just walked right over and joined him. I was mad at myself for not getting Divafied this morning, but even without it, I was still a bad bitch!

"Hi, beautiful. Thanks for coming."

"You're welcome. What's up?"

"Nothing, I'm getting ready to hit the road and for some reason, I couldn't leave without seeing you. Ever since that night at the club, I've been thinking about what could've been between us, you know?"

I was totally speechless. I self-consciously started toying with my wedding ring.

"Malik, I'm married."

"Wow, when did that happen?"

"Not too long ago."

"Well, why did you come here, Sasha? Obviously, you're not happy."

It was at that moment that I realized that we were sitting at the same table that Sean proposed to me at. The tears started to flow without my consent. I don't know why, but I felt torn between what was me and Sean, and what could be of Malik and me. I knew it was wrong to feel that way, but my heart couldn't tell a lie. Malik grabbed my face and gently kissed my lips while wiping my tears away.

At that moment, I felt ashamed of myself but revived at the same time. I felt alive again, and I wanted to remain in his kiss forever. My heart stopped beating momentarily when he pulled away, and I was at a loss for words.

"Leave that nigga and all the dope boy shit, and come with me so I can show you how you should be treated."

"You don't know shit about how we're living. He does treat me good, Malik," I said, getting defensive. He hit the table so hard I jumped.

"Bullshit, ma! I hear shit! Just because I'm not in the streets no more, I still keep my ear to them. Look at you, all bruised up and shit!"

I was so embarrassed at that point. I didn't think they were that noticeable on my dark skin.

"Malik, I'm sorry, but I think I should go."

I went to stand and he grabbed my hand. "Sasha, wait!" I stood there for a minute, fighting back the rest of my tears.

"What, Malik? I have to go."

"I know. I just wanted to give you my number before I left."

"For what, Malik?"

"Anything ma, even if it's just to talk. I'll always be here for you, no matter what. Just because you don't want me as your man doesn't mean that we can't still be friends, does it?"

"No, you're right. Here," I said as I handed him my phone.

He stored his number in and said, "Wait, one more thing."

"Yes, Malik?"

"I just wanted to say that I'm very sorry for your loss."

I leaned down and kissed his cheek and said thank you, and then I swiftly walked away.

LORD FORGIVE ME,
FOR I HAVE SINNED AGAIN

I was posted up outside of one of the strip clubs in College Park. I had rented a room at the Marriott and chilled all day with my phone off so I could get my mind right for tonight. I was driving Sean's black Camaro that I had gone home and jumped in once I knew that he was gone. I had all of my black attire on, including a pair of Sean's black leather gloves that I'd stolen from his closet earlier.

I had been sitting there since 11:00 p.m., and it was now 1:30. The club closed at 2:00, so it was now or never. Luckily for me, the club was packed, so this dumb hoe had parked on a side street next to the club. I started the car, drove around a couple of blocks, and parked in the projects. I got out and tucked my Ginsu knife into my sleeve. I ran back to her car and realized that she hadn't even locked the doors, which I was pretty prepared to pop. I looked around to make sure the coast was clear, opened the back door of the Taurus, and slid in. I laid there patiently waiting, thinking about Kash and my reasons for doing what I was about to do when the door opened and she slid in. Just as she closed the door, I sprang up and put my hand over her mouth and my blade across her throat.

In one swift motion, I cut so deep into her throat that I hit the bone, then I whispered, "Bitch, now you know how it feels to choke on your own blood and die, just like my daughter did!"

I wiped the bloody blade on her shirt, cautiously slipped back out, sprinted to my car, and drove off. I got home before Sean, thank God, and stripped naked in the garage and threw everything into our incinerator like I had seen Sean do before. I put my clothes from earlier back on, went into the house, soaked the knife in bleach, and put it back up. I hurriedly grabbed the keys to my car and put Sean's back, then I jumped in my whip and headed back to the hotel for the night.

I still had Plies' song, "All Black" that I was listening to on the way to the club stuck in my head. I was just like Queen Latifah in "Set it Off" when it came to riding music. The song had to always fit the occasion. When I got back to the hotel, I decided to call Sean. He picked up on the first ring.

"Yo, where are you at, Sash?"

"I'm at a hotel. Where are you at?"

"I'm riding around picking up this money. When do you plan on coming home?"

"I don't know. I got a lot of shit on my mind right now that I need to sort out first."

"Alright, well I ain't gonna stress you, Ma. When you are ready, I'll be there."

I sighed in relief, thankful that he wasn't trying to argue.

"Sasha?"

"Yeah, I'm here."

"I love you, and I want you to forgive me. I don't wanna fight no more, baby. Get yo mind right and come on home."

"I love you too, Sean. Goodnight."

I hung and unpacked my gold and purple panther print sequin Bettysville overnight bag. I took a shower to rinse the stench of death off of my body and soul. I had committed a sin, but I felt no remorse at all for the murder I had just done. I smiled at the thought of that bitch being six feet deep. She didn't deserve to breathe the same air as me. There was now one less hood rat in the world if you asked me. I did feel slightly bad because her kids wouldn't have a mother but hell, look at the pain she caused my baby, and she felt no remorse. When I was done showering, I slipped into my Victoria's Secret Very Sexy tank and panty set and sprayed on some of the matching body spray. I got under the covers of the king sized bed and snuggled into the plush king pillows. I closed my eyes and said my prayers.

"Father, forgive me, for I have sinned. Now I lay me down to sleep. I pray the Lord my soul to keep. If I should die before I wake, I pray the Lord my soul to take."

I awoke to the vibrating of my phone.

"Hello?"

"Did I wake you?"

"No, I was just laying here."

"Oh. Well, can you talk or is this a bad time?"

"Yeah, I can talk. What's up?

"Well, I'm flying out today and I was wondering if we could do breakfast?"

"Yes, if you come up to the Marriott where I'm staying, and

we can order some room service."

"Cool, which one?"

I gave him the location and the room number. As soon as I hung up, I jumped out of the bed and raced into the bathroom. I quickly brushed my teeth, brushed my hair, and freshened up a bit. I glossed my lips, then went over to the nightstand and dialed up room service. I looked at the clock and it was only 8:30. I sat down on the bed, feeling guilty for what I was doing; but was I really doing anything wrong? I mean yeah, I loved Sean; but at the same time, I felt like this relationship wasn't going anywhere.

Shit, we had separate goals and wanted different things out of life. I wanted the happily ever after, the kids and the white picket fence, love, trust and a committed husband. All he wanted was to do was chase women and get money. I couldn't help but wonder if maybe I could have all those things with Malik. No matter how hard I tried not to feel guilty, I did.

I picked up my phone to call Malik and tell him not to come. As soon as I hit talk, there was a knock at the door. Damn, I was too late! I hung up and let him in. He just stood there and let his eyes roam my body, from my pedicured toes to my ample breasts.

"Are you going to just stand there, or are you going to come in?"

He came in and laid across my bed. I got under the covers and patted the spot next to me. He kicked off his shoes, scooted up, and got under the covers next to me. We sat and talked until our food came. We ate and talked some more. For some reason, I was telling him things that I wasn't even comfortable talking to Sean about. We talked about Kash, my prison time, his family, and our goals in life.

Even though the sexual tension was higher than a crackhead on SSI around the first of the month, I couldn't help but wonder if Sean felt this way around his side chicks. I was still sleepy and emotionally drained, but I didn't want him to go just yet. I snuggled up to him and he wrapped his arms around me. We laid there silently enjoying each other's company until I fell asleep.

When I woke up two hours later, he was gone. I had to wonder if I had dreamed it all. My phone vibrated, signaling that I had a text message.

It read, "Hey beautiful, I hope you slept good. Now go home and try to make amends with ya man and if it don't work out, holla at ya boy!"

My heart smiled. He was so sweet. I decided to follow his advice. I got up and threw on my clothes, tidied up, packed, and headed home to try and work on fixing my marriage. They say that most marriages fail within the first three years and I didn't want to become a statistic!

As I was getting in my car, my cell phone rang. It was Shawni.

"What up, fool?"

"Girl, you ain't gonna believe this shit, but I'm going to tell you anyway!"

"Well, spill it already!" By then, I was on my way out of the parking lot.

"Girl, I was watching the news this morning and Amaris' face was all over the screen. She was murdered last night!"

"Yeah, I know."

"Damn, how you know, because I know you don't watch the news?"

"Now you're talking too much. You aren't 5-0 are you?" I asked playfully.

"Bitch, please! I know you better than you know yourself, and your name is written all over this one!"

"It's not what you know, but what you can prove. Now, goodbye!"

"Bye."

GUCCI GIRL

Things were strained a little with Sean, but we were still working at it. In addition, yes, I had still been conversing with Malik on a regular basis. It was only a little friendly chatter here and there. For some reason, he was the only person who brought positivity to my life. Sean was always on the grind, Shawni was so busy with the shop, and she and Todd were contemplating settling down together. I know—Shawni settling down, yeah right, but it was true. My baby sis was finally maturing.

It was a bright sunny Saturday morning, and Sean was headed to New York on some business.

"Hey Sasha, you done packing my bag? I gotta go before I miss my flight."

"Yeah, boo. I miss you already and you're not even gone yet."

"Aww, don't worry. A week ain't shit. I'll be back before you know it," he said and kissed my lips.

I got dressed in a pair of black Cavalli skinny jeans, a white and black Just Cavalli tank top, and some zebra print with the red stiletto Jimmy Choos. I pulled my hair up into a sleek ponytail and applied my Urban Decay cosmetics, glossed my lips, and hit the door. I was on my way to the Underground Station for a little retail therapy and excitement.

As I walked through the mall drinking a strawberry kiwi smoothie, a white guy about 30ish approached me.

"Excuse me, miss?"

I pulled my Chanel shades up and said, "Yes? Can I help you?"

"Yes, I think you can. My name is Jameson Whitmore, and I am a scout from High Class Modeling Agency for Gucci. I'm looking for someone for our next campaign, and I think I've found her!"

"Is this some kind of scam? Shit, this is Atlanta and everybody got a hustle!"

"No ma'am. I'm legit. Here's my card."

"Okay, what's the catch?"

"There is no catch. Just meet me at the office on that card tomorrow at 9:00 a.m. sharp, and we can go over the details."

"Oh. I'll think about it."

"Thank you for your time, and I hope to see you in the morning."

"Yeah, maybe," I said as I walked away.

I couldn't believe it. Hopefully, he was serious. Shit, as much Gucci as me and Sean rocked, I just ought to! I was so excited that I couldn't sleep that night. I didn't tell anyone just in case it fell through. I got up and showered. I kept it simple and classic with the makeup, then I picked out a black pencil skirt and a short-sleeved blazer with some silver Prada peep toes, and silver hoop earrings. By 8:00, I was out the door and pulled out of my driveway. I let the navigation system in the Lex lead the way. An hour later and $10,000 richer, with a contract and check in hand, I was one of the five new faces of Gucci globally! I called everybody in my family to share the good news. They were so happy for me; then, I called Sean.

The first thing he said was, "You don't need to work. We got money."

He just didn't get it sometimes. Yeah, we had money, but it wasn't about the money. I needed an identity, a legacy to leave my children. I needed a sense of being. This gave me hope. I needed a purpose, and this was only the beginning. I hoped it was going to open up a lot of doors for me!

For the next couple of weeks, I was so busy. I flew all over the country doing different photo shoots. It was amazing! After all the wrong I had done, God was still showing me favor. Sometimes, Sean came with me. Even though he didn't say it, I could see it in his eyes. He was happy for me. He supported me every step of the way. I think he was finally seeing life through my eyes—through the eyes of the world. They even invited him to one of my shoots in New York. He obliged and even thought about getting his own portfolio done. We were finally getting on the same page. When you owned businesses, that was only material stuff.

I started a charity and bought and opened a center for troubled teen girls and runaways. I hired mentors. It had lavish bedrooms. I also hired a couple of therapists and a social worker. We fed, clothed, and nurtured troubled female youth. I was very hands-on with this project, so instead of blowing more money on things I didn't need, I gave back to the community.

Within the next year, I would be opening another center in my hometown of Saginaw, Michigan. This was just a start. Eventually, Girl Genius would open up sites all over the nation. Thanks to modeling, my dreams were becoming a reality! Now that I had a career and my life back, I could start working on that white picket fence and children.

Sean was thinking about finally going legit. It was something I'd been nagging him about for months now. We had millions and eventually, greed was gonna come knocking on our door. I tried to tell him to let the game go now because I was sure there were niggas gunning for his spot and waiting on him to slip up. Even though we had our moments, I loved him and I wasn't ready to lose him to the streets. He was a street nigga, and that was all he knew, and I felt it was my duty as his wife to expose him to better.

WE BE CLUBBING

When we arrived in Miami, it was beautiful to say the least! I had a bikini photo shoot for Gucci. I had my sister with me, and we were geeked up! I got Shawni settled in at the hotel and was off to a brief prepping. When I was done, I went back to the hotel to get some rest so I would be on point for my shoot in the morning. We watched a movie and ate fresh fruit, drank a couple of coolers, and then called it a night. The next morning, we were chauffeured to the location in a black on black Maybach. We felt like stars!

For the next two days, it was all business. I did so many wardrobe changes that I lost count. My favorite was the fuchsia Gucci logo two-piece with some fuchsia Gucci pumps and gold-rimmed fuchsia lensed oversized shades with the logo monogrammed in. I was looking like new money! My hair was bone straight and blowing in the wind. Shawni was so encouraging and supportive. I loved her for that. She was my rock and vice-versa. She was the Betty to my Wilma and down to walk, ride, or run with me barefoot.

The last day of the shoot was the most exhausting. I was drained but afterward, we were treated to a four-course meal at a five-star restaurant along the beach. When we were all stuffed, we went back to the hotel and got dressed for the Miami Heat game they were also treating us to. We had seats in the skybox.

"Yo Sis, I might have to rethink this relationship thing and snag me one of these ballers up in here tonight!"

"Girl, you know Todd would kill you and that nigga first!"

We laughed and mingled with some of the players' wives. We sipped mojitos and drank champagne. I started feeling nauseated, so we called it a night as soon as the game was over. I thought I had been overexerting myself lately. I stayed tired and didn't have much of an appetite. I needed some time off, and planned to take it in the near future. I had to rest up because next fall, my Genius Girl collection would be coming out, and I had to be ready. I knew that between that, modeling, and the center, I would be working like crazy. The girls were excited and I refused to let them down. They had been working so hard on helping me design the clothing line, and I was going to make sure that they got their shine on. They were also going to be the models for the runway show and ads.

The next morning when we walked out of the hotel, the Maybach was right there waiting. We hit up all the boutiques and bought everything from Chanel to Prada and Dior! Hell, my black card didn't have a limit, so why should we?

Next, we got massages and Brazilian waxes. We strolled the beach and flirted with hot guys and just had fun! By sunset, we were still all the way live! Once we returned to our hotel, we tipped the driver and told him to give us an hour and a half. We were ready in a flash. We stood side by side in the mirror admiring ourselves. I was rocking a colorful strapless Chanel dress that fit my curves like it was painted on, stopping right above my knee. The shoes were turquoise wraparounds. My makeup was flawless, like my Chanel jewelry. Shawni had on some blue Dior booty shorts with an off the shoulder matching top, silver Giuseppe heels, and silver Tiffany jewelry.

We grabbed our purses and hit the town. The stars were shining, and it was a full moon. I called Sean on the way out.

"Hey, babe!"

"What's up bae, yawl enjoying yourselves?"

"And you know it! We are out here doing it big!"

"I just bet yawl are."

"Well, I was just checking in. I miss you."

"I miss you too, ma. And don't forget to scoop me up something dope."

"I won't. Love you, babe."

"Love you too, Sash. Have fun and be safe."

"Okay. Bye."

"Bye, babe."

"Aww ain't yawl cute?"

"Shut up, Shawni! You are just jealous."

"I know. Let me call Todd."

By the time she ended her conversation, we were pulling up to our first club. As soon as we walked into the club, it was all eyes on us. They were banging Trina's "White Girl" through the speakers and we sashayed straight to the dance floor. We hit all the hottest spots in Miami. By 2:00 a.m., I was ready to call it a night. I think I overdid it with the Cristal because I felt sick as a dog. I guess that's what I get since I said I was done drinking that shit because they were so called racist, but I was not about to turn down nothing but my collar from these niggas. I didn't have to open my wallet all night.

When we got into the room, I didn't even bother getting undressed. I just crawled into bed and held my stomach until I fell asleep, shoes and all. The next morning, I was awakened by the vomit threatening its way up my throat. I jumped up and ran to the bathroom. I barely got my face over the toilet bowl before it came splashing out of my mouth. I threw up off and on for about an hour. I guess I woke Shawni up because when I pulled my head out for the umpteenth time, she appeared in the doorway.

"Bitch, you pregnant ain't you?"

"I don't know, but something is wrong with me."

"Ooh, I'm telling Mama!"

"Girl, I'm grown! And you better not tell her until I know for sure."

Once I ate some crackers and ginger ale, I felt a little better. I refused to eat or drink anything else. We stayed in all day and relaxed.

Luckily for me, I had grabbed Sean some Gucci short sets and Gucci shades from one of the shoots. I know, but they were free. That is one of the many perks of my job, so why not?

The next morning, we were on a plane headed home. First stop, a drugstore.

As soon as Sean saw me, he knew something wrong. I assured him that I would be just fine after some Thera-Flu and some rest.

He took us to the drugstore after we left the airport. I grabbed two pregnancy tests and some Thera-Flu to make it look good. I paid for my things and threw the tests in my purse. When I got to the car, Shawni and Sean were laughing and talking about some of the stuff we saw while in Miami. I just rested my head on the headrest, trying to relax. The anticipation was killing me. Sean grabbed my hand and held it as we dropped Ashawni off. He held it the rest of the way home.

I was glad to be home. I missed my man more than I thought. His touch was so soothing, even though I was feeling like shit.

"I love you, Sean."

"I love you too, babe. Just relax and let daddy take care of you."

I smiled in compliance.

GOING IN CIRCLES

As soon as I stepped off the plane in Detroit, I was greeted by my assistant, Esha. She helped me work my center in Saginaw. She cut right to the chase, briefing me for all of my meetings and contracts. First stop would be my brother's house. His girlfriend Samara had a meal prepared for me, and I couldn't wait to sink my teeth into it. The two-hour ride from Detroit to Saginaw flashed before my eyes due to the fact that Esha had so much to tell me in so little time.

Once I reached his house, I took a hot bath and put on some jogging pants and a t-shirt. I kicked it with my family for a couple of hours and caught up on current events. I retreated to the guest room at about 10:00 p.m. and called it a night. I had a big, busy day tomorrow.

I was up early the next morning. I wanted to go see some of my other family members. I had breakfast with them, and then I left and made my rounds. Afterward, I headed to the center. It was beautiful. It was located on Michigan street, which was between the inner city and the township. I had it built from the ground up. It had a state of the art kitchen, a family room, and a game room. There were 20 individual bedrooms with private bathrooms and a media room. I had security guards and monitors along with staff 24 hours a day. I was so amazed with the job that the contractors and the interior decorator had done. My vision was now a reality.

I attended all of my meetings, made new contacts, and

bumped shoulders with some of the wealthiest people in the city, who were also trying to invest in my project. I had turned my life around so tremendously in so little time that I had to pat myself on the back. I was even trying to stop cursing altogether. I had kicked my recreational cocaine habit, and was now pregnant for the second time. Yeah, Shawni was right! I hoped this pregnancy was going to be different. I couldn't go through another tragedy.

It was 4:45 p.m., and the mayor and News 5 had just arrived for the ribbon cutting ceremony. After the ribbon was cut, we had finger foods, champagne, and various chocolates. At about 8:00pm, I got a frantic call from Shawni saying that Sean had been shot and robbed about an hour ago! I located my assistant and had her get me on the first flight she could. I said my goodbyes and abruptly left.

It felt like my driver was moving at a snail's pace. I was trying to keep my composure. I had four hours until the next flight anyway. I put on my iPod and tried to relax. That was the wrong move because the first song that came on was Jordin Sparks' "No Air." The floodgates behind my eyelids opened. I wanted to be mad at Sean for constantly pulling us backward, but I couldn't because he was who he was and the man I had fallen in love with. I guess just because I'd changed, I was wrong for expecting him to change too.

Once we reached the airport, I sat and waited an hour and a half before I got out of the luxury truck. I had composed myself greatly. I took a Xanax and slept through most of the flight.

Shawni was waiting for me at the airport as soon as I arrived.

As soon as we got into the car, she gave me the rundown on Sean. I wouldn't allow her to earlier. I had too long of a way to go before I could get here for any added stress.

"Girl, stop worrying, he's okay. It went straight through his left leg, so he's going to be okay.

"Oh, thank God! Shawni, I'm so tired of worrying about that man that I could scream! And by the way, I'm pregnant."

"Sasha, I already knew that! I told you and Mama!"

"I can't stand your tattle-telling butt!"

"I know, right? You know I can't hold water!"

I walked into the hospital and was greeted by half of Sean's family. They briefed me on his condition and told me his room number. My husband looked so peaceful lying there asleep.

I walked up to him and whispered, "Wake up, boo," softly in his ear.

He opened his eyes and smiled. "How was your grand opening, baby?"

"It was fine. But more importantly, how are you?"

"I'm good. They said I can leave within the next couple of days."

"Alright, well I'm going home to change and I'll be back to keep you company."

"Take your time, Sash. I ain't going nowhere."

"I love you, Sean."

"I love you too babe, and for what it's worth, I'm sorry for ruining one of the best days of your life. I know how much it meant to you."

"Thanks," I said as I walked out the door.

TIL DEATH DO US PART

I was on my way to my first doctor's appointment. I was happy and nervous at the same time. I didn't know how far along I was or anything. I know that's some trifling stuff, but I just had so many loose ends to tie up before I settled down. My life had been hectic lately. Sean had recovered completely, with a slight limp. I was now on vacation from modeling, and the centers were running smoothly. The shop was Shawni's responsibility now. Therefore, I could now put the focus on myself.

I found out that I was four and a half months pregnant! I was barely showing and had only gained ten pounds. My doctor told me to eat more and cut back on some of my cardio. He also gave me a prescription for some prenatal vitamins. As soon as I got home, I called Sean to tell him how my appointment went and the other great news that I had received. I didn't even give him the chance to say hello!

"Hey, baby! Guess what?"

"What, miss happy go lucky?"

"We're having twins!"

"What? Are you serious, girl?"

"I'm dead-ass serious! And there's a boy and a girl!"

"Damn, Sasha! You just made me happier than a trick in a house full of hoes!"

"Boy, you stupid! Hurry home so we can celebrate!"

"Okay. Give me a couple of hours."

Two hours later, I had set up a candlelight lasagna dinner with fresh green beans, salad, and dinner rolls. I poured two glasses of wine and waited. Sorry to say, I ate alone. By the time Sean got home, it was 2 a.m.

"Sasha, you awake?"

"I am now."

"I'm sorry, but I had something came up that had to be handled right away."

"Yeah, well your food is in the fridge."

I said goodnight and turned over and went back to sleep. Two weeks later, I received a call from the doctor's office telling me that I needed to come in ASAP to discuss the results of my bloodwork. I headed straight over there. I thought something was wrong with my babies. After checking in, I was led straight back. After sitting in a room for about ten minutes, in came my doctor.

The news he gave me was devastating. He said that I was HIV positive! How could this happen? I was a good person! Yeah, I made some mistakes in life, but I was only human! I swear this was karma coming back for me with a vengeance.

I didn't even remember driving home. I closed all of the blinds, took two Xanax, and went to bed. What was I going to do? My life was now ruined. I truly hated Sean!

I was now realizing that my love for him was killing me. I knew he would be my death sentence, but my heart just couldn't let him go.

When I loved, I loved hard, and it cost me my sanity and my

life. There was no way that I could live with this disease. My poor babies what about them? Even if they made it, who was going to raise them? Luckily, I had a great family. Between Ashawni and my mom, they would be alright.

I called Sean several times in a panic. He never answered. He was not here for me as usual; this was becoming a once a week routine. The next morning, I woke up to Sean pulling down my panties. I hadn't even heard him come in the night before. I laid there and went through the motions as I let him undress me. He rolled over on his back and pulled me on top of him. As I rode him with no emotion, I remembered the .380 he always kept under his pillow.

He was so gone off the sex that he didn't even realize I was now pointing it at his face. When he opened his eyes, they bucked as my rhythm slowed and my tears dripped onto his chest while I held the gun.

"Sasha, what are you doing?"

"Shut up Sean, it's your entire fault!"

"What baby, what did I do?"

"What did you do? You gave me HIV—that is what you did! Now I am four and a half months pregnant with HIV!

"Baby, I am so sorry," he said as he tried to grab the gun.

Boom, boom, boom were the last sounds I heard before I collapsed onto his chest. Our hearts beat as one. I killed my husband, my love, my life, my air. I was suffocating. Jordin Sparks' song started playing over and over in my head.

"If I should die before I wake, it's 'cause you took my breath away. Losing you is like living in the world with no air!"

I was still holding the smoking gun as I prayed for my babies. My hand was violently shaking as I put the gun to my temple...

Made in the USA
Lexington, KY
27 April 2017